*SCENE*

Within microseconds, Rod had seen the attack and recognized it for what it was: an assassination attempt. He vaulted from the car into the road and landed in a crouch, spinning to face a motorcycle. Rod reached out and steel-cored fingers bit into the driver's helmet, puncturing the fiberglass. He yanked hard and flipped the motorcyclist off the back of the bike, neck broken by the impact.

Another motorcycle had been holding back. Its driver gunned the engine and it hurtled up from the rear, the rider crouched low as he leveled his gun at Rod. The robot's senses detected the bullets as they snapped past, registering position, velocity, and trajectory.

Rod whirled as something slammed into his left arm. He had been keeping an automatic tally of the enemies and thought that all were accounted for. But then two 9mm rounds had just struck him in the left arm, blows that tore cloth and synthetic plastic skin. He tracked the path of the rounds back to an FBI agent with an Uzi.

CYBERNARC

ROBERT CAIN

HarperPaperbacks
A Division of HarperCollinsPublishers

HarperPaperbacks   *A Division of* HarperCollins*Publishers*
10 East 53rd Street, New York, N.Y. 10022

Copyright © 1991 by HarperCollins*Publishers*
All rights reserved. No part of this book may be used or reproduced in any manner whatsoever without written permission of the publisher, except in the case of brief quotations embodied in critical articles and reviews. For information address HarperCollins*Publishers*, 10 East 53rd Street, New York, N.Y. 10022.

Cover illustration by Rick Nemo

First printing: August 1991

Printed in the United States of America

HarperPaperbacks and colophon are trademarks of HarperCollins*Publishers*

10 9 8 7 6 5 4 3 2 1

◐ Prologue

THEY CALLED HIM ROD.

He did not understand that the name was derived from the name of the Rand Corporation project that had created him. Indeed, it could not be said that he *understood* anything at all, at least, not in the human sense.

Rod was not human.

Not yet.

Vision check, a voice said in his head. *Focus.*

Grid lines superimposed themselves on his unblinking view of Lab One. The words DIAGNOSTIC MODE: VISUAL winked on at the periphery of his vision, not for his benefit but for that of the human technicians who were now seeing through his camera eyes. A man's face appeared for a moment, close up and distorted by the wide-angle effect. A hand blotted out the lab panorama as the technician made a minute adjustment to the locking ring behind Rod's left eye. The image blurred, then sharpened.

"Focus okay," his own voice replied as face and hand pulled back. It was baritone, male, and perfectly human.

Telescopic, the voice in his head ordered.

1

Crosshairs replaced the focus grid. The scene shifted as a human controller turned Rod's head and raised it, centering his view on three Rand scientists standing on the far side of the lab. They were watching themselves on a large wall screen that displayed what Rod saw.

With a tiny whirr, the image expanded, numerals indicating range, focal length, and magnification flickering at the lower right. The scene zoomed in on the figure of Dr. Heather McDaniels, closing in first on her upper body, then on her left breast, finally focusing on the faintly shadowed outline of her nipple where it pressed against her blouse.

Enhance.

Wrinkles in the shiny white fabric sharpened. The shadow darkened, stretching the contrast and delineating the nipple.

"Very funny, Greg," McDaniels's voice said sharply. The image blurred and changed as she moved. "Juvenile, but very funny."

"Telescopic enhancement satisfactory," Rod said matter-of-factly. Though he sensed irritation in McDaniels's voice and could read through his thermal sensors the slight increase in skin temperature on her face and throat, the meaning of her words was lost to him.

Nor did he understand the laughs from several of the men in the room. Greg Irvin chuckled. "Way to go, Rod. You're getting more human every day!"

"Wait until he has a gun in his hand," another voice said. "Then we'll see how human he is."

Rod had not heard that voice before, but the probability exceeded seventy percent that the newcomer was the man who had checked in through RAMROD security ninety-two minutes earlier. Rod accessed the file from personnel, letting the data flicker through his awareness. Christopher C. Drake. U.S. Navy SEAL lieutenant, active duty, temporary attached duty to RAMROD, seconded from Joint Special Operations Command with security clearance Blue Five, service number . . .

"You don't think Rod can perform as advertised, Lieutenant?" James Weston, the head of Project RAMROD, stepped into view. With him was a man in navy dress blues whose face matched the ID photo in Chris Drake's file.

"Aw, come on, Mr. Weston," Drake replied. "It takes a hell of a lot more than a science-fiction writer's nightmare to function in combat! How do you teach a *machine* to pick up a gun, pick out the bad guys from the good guys, aim—"

"Hell, just *recognizing* a gun is a challenge for an AI program," Weston said. "But you're thinking of Apple IIs or a SuperCray. Rod here doesn't process information like that."

"Terrific. You still can't make a soldier, not like that. You have to *grow* him, with discipline, training, and one hell of a lot of experience!"

Weston laughed. "And that, Lieutenant Drake, is precisely why we sent for you. You have the experience our friend here needs."

Rod recognized the expression on Drake's face as a frown but did not understand why it was there.

● Chapter One

WITH SCARCELY A STIR in the ferns or rotting vegetation to mark their cautious movements, the raiders lay on the mountain's jungle-covered slope, watching. Wearing camouflage fatigues and floppy-brimmed, jungle boonie hats, their faces and hands smeared with green, they were all but invisible against shadows growing rapidly blacker as the early-evening light faded from the sky.

Five of the six raiders crouching in the darkness were U.S. Navy SEALs, HALOed into their mountain-valley DZ early that morning. They weren't supposed to be there, of course. Their silenced weapons, combat dress, and equipment had all been carefully sanitized so that the State Department and the Pentagon could deny that the raiders had any connection at all with the elite military covert operations team.

The sixth man, a field agent assigned by the DEA attaché in Bogotá, had met them at the DZ and led them to the jungle OP overlooking their objective.

The site gave them a clear line of sight over the south wall of a sprawling country estate. The main house was a two-story, U-shaped mansion of white stucco with red-

4

tiled roofing. By the east wing, where pool and patio, overlooked by a railed, second-floor wooden deck, nestled among flowers and ornamental hedges, dozens of people gathered, the women in pastel gowns, the men in formal white or black tuxedos. Party lanterns and the shimmering reflections from the pool's underwater lights gave the assembly a festive air.

The estate grounds, from the coast road to the ten-meter cliff above the Caribbean surf, were completely surrounded by a three-meter wall. Paramilitary types wearing fatigues and carrying assault rifles checked each carload of guests as they turned off the coast road and approached the main gate. More guests were arriving minute by minute, many in expensive-looking cars with the low-slung manner that suggested heavy armor.

Eight hundred meters to the south, the SEALs watched and recorded the scene. Lieutenant Christopher Drake lay on his belly and peered through the covering vegetation, the earphone of a radio headset pressed against one ear. A few meters to the right, MM/2 Kaminski sighted through the eyepiece of a tripod-mounted starlight camera, while RN/3 Timmons crouched nearby at the terminal of the team's satellite ground station. The AN/TSC-124's dish antenna was already unfolded and aligned with a MILSTAR satellite in the sky some eleven degrees south of the zenith and slightly to the west. Two more SEALs were out of sight in the jungle, providing flank security.

"C'mon . . . c'mon . . ." Lieutenant Drake could hear nothing but dead air over the headphone. There were no transmissions at all on the assigned frequency. "Where the hell's your spook, Esposito?"

"Be cool," responded the camo-clad man lying at Drake's side. He squinted through the eyepiece of a starlight scope. "He's here. *Trust* me."

Drake scowled, the expression masked by darkness and the camo paint on his face. "Trust me." Right.

He detested the bureaucratic infighting that characterized multidepartmental operations. He didn't know Esposito, and on an op like this he wasn't ready to trust him with anything more demanding than opening a can of beer. Damn it, the man wasn't even a SEAL!

According to the mission briefings, SNOWDROP was supposed to provide a communications relay for a DEA undercover agent, code-named "Gator," among the party's guests. Unfortunately, the whole op had the familiar air of a poorly conceived, spur-of-the-moment brainstorm by some desk-jockeying suit back in Washington. It looked to Drake like he had been yanked from his billet in Project RAMROD for no better reason than that the Drug Enforcement Administration had given Emilio Esposito the courtesy rank of lieutenant, and Drake's superiors were unwilling to have one of their teams commanded by a non-SEAL officer.

La Fortaleza Salazar. That was what the estate below the SEAL OP was called. One of several homes owned by the patriarch of the powerful Salazar family, the mansion and grounds were small by the standards of Colombia's wealthy elite, but it embraced several dozen choice acres along the coastline a few miles east of Santa Marta. An airfield complete with warehouses and a 1,200-meter landing strip had been constructed a kilometer farther to the east.

During the daytime, the vista must be spectacular.

Jungle and tangled tropical vegetation predominated along the coast; only forty-five kilometers to the south Bolivia's two highest peaks, eternally snow-clad Colón and Bolívar, reached an elevation of almost 5,800 meters. And to the north lay the azure waters of the Caribbean.

The region was also one of the country's most dangerous. Colombia's north coast had long been prime marijuana-growing country, but during the past ten years cannabis had given way to the far more profitable coca leaf. The coast from Santa Marta to Rio Hacha was all but owned outright by the drug lords who constituted Colombia's second, secret government.

Operation SNOWDROP had been conceived as a combined effort by the Drug Enforcement Administration and the U.S. Joint Special Operations Command, working under the umbrella of Group Seven, the President's special antinarcotics advisory task force. During the past several years, there'd been a number of such covert insertions by U.S. combat teams into Colombia and other South American countries. The w. r on drugs was coming to a boil, and the American combatants, the DEA and JSOC among them, were finding themselves in greater and greater need of precise and up-to-date intelligence.

Suddenly Drake heard a click in his earpiece, then a burst of static. "Peeping Tom, Peeping Tom," a muffled voice said. "This is Gator. Hope you boys're out there and got your ears on."

"Got him!" Drake adjusted the gain on the receiver. "He's transmitting."

The signal was weak but clear. Gator was wearing

a tiny radio transmitter wired into his bridgework. The range of the device was sharply limited—a few dozen meters—but a more powerful transceiver and micro-miniaturized power pack had been built into an expensive-looking fountain pen. Gator was supposed to plant the pen somewhere on the estate grounds where the SEALs in the hills to the south would have it in their line of sight. So long as the DEA agent was within range of the pen, the SEALs would be able to listen in on what he heard, as well as pick up his running, underbreath commentary.

"Just dropped the pen in the potted palms," Gator continued. "If you're where you're supposed to be, you should have a good signal."

At his side, Esposito stiffened, then adjusted the zoom on his LI scope. "I see him. By the door to the patio."

"Friend of yours?" Drake asked. He signaled to Timmons, who flicked a switch on the AN/TSC terminal. Gator's words would be heard and recorded by the SIGINT boys back at Fort Meade.

Esposito shook his head. "No. Never met him. He's been undercover here quite a while, getting in solid with the Salazars. He was the one who alerted Washington that this drug-lord summit was going down."

Most of the bosses of Colombia's drug cartels were expected to be here tonight. No one knew what the meet was about, exactly, but the DEA wanted a photographic record of the party and its guests. And Gator would be on hand to provide a running commentary through the bug in his teeth. He was present as a guest of his very good friend, José Gonzalo Salazar-Aria.

According to the mission briefing, José Salazar, nick-named *El Tiburón,* "The Shark," was one of the king-pins of the Colombian cocaine trade. His uncle, Roberto Augusto Salazar-Mendoza, was the aging patriarch of the Salazar clan and the owner of the seacoast estate.

Esposito shifted in the darkness. "I can't get a clear view," he whispered.

Drake heard the rustle of vegetation as the DEA agent changed positions. Silly bastard, he thought. God help them all if this amateur gave the SEALs away. Fortunately, the night sounds of the jungle—a cacophony of keeking, chirruping, and peeping from frogs and in-sects—enveloped them, as much a part of their cover as the black vegetation around them. He ignored the man and concentrated on Gator's transmission.

"Okay, boys and girls," the undercover agent was saying. The words were slurred and indistinct, the re-sult of his having to mumble under his breath. Drake had to strain to distinguish them. "I'm on the patio now. Looks like a Who's Who of the local cartels. I'm standing about twenty feet from *El Padrino,* Pablo Es-cobar Gaviria. Yellow shirt, heavy mustache. Over there helping himself to the buffet is Roberto Augusto Salazar. Old, dignified-looking guy with white hair.

"Good God, there's Don Fabio himself! Fabio Ochoa, godfather of the whole damned Ochoa clan . . . he's the guy who looks like a walking ton of lard talking to Roberto. Something about Ochoa's string of horses.

"Shit! Hold it a sec. Company coming."

"Señor Patiño!" a new voice interrupted. *"Cómo está?"*

Drake spoke fluent Spanish, one of the reasons he'd

been pulled for SNOWDROP. Felíx Patiño, he knew, was Gator's cover name with the Colombian drug lords.

"Señor García!" Gator said, the words suddenly loud and sharp, almost shouted in the SEAL's ear as the agent spoke aloud for the first time. *"Estoy bien. Qué pasa?"*

"We need to talk," García said. "Now. Inside, with your permission, señor?"

Kaminski looked up from his camera. "They're going back inside."

"Signal's still clear," Drake said. The miniature transmitter would have pretty fair penetration inside the house, so long as Gator didn't wander too far from the fountain-pen relay on the patio.

"Well, Felíx," a new voice said over the bug, this time in English. "Time for your amusing charade to end."

"José?" Gator's voice sounded strained. "Hey, man! What's with all the guns?"

"Qué?" another voice asked. Evidently not everyone in the room spoke English. *"Qué pasa, Señor Salazar?"*

"This pig works undercover for the DEA," José Salazar replied in Spanish. "Take him."

"Hey, man!" Gator's voice cracked. "Hey, no . . . Listen! Who gave you that undercover shit, José? It ain't true!"

"Save your breath, Felíx . . . or whatever your real name is. And don't expect help from your friends in the jungle. We know about them as well."

"I don't know what you're talking about, man!" The voice was shrill now. "I'm no spy! You *invited* me here!"

"I'm told he has a small radio concealed in his teeth," Salazar said. "Eduardo? Why don't we see if we can find it? The butt of your rifle should do nicely."

"No! Please, *no*—" There was a sickening crunch, followed by a burst of static.

"Shit!" Drake whipped the headset off. "Time to abort! Damn it, where's Esposito."

The DEA agent reappeared out of the darkness. "What is it? What happened?"

"We're *burned*, Lieutenant!" Drake unslung his silenced Uzi subgun and jerked the bolt back, chambering a round. "From the sound of things they've already called in the cavalry!" He pressed the earplug of the small personal communicator he wore under his boonie hat and adjusted the lip mike. "Flanker!" he called. "This is Drop Leader. You got any movement out there?"

"Nada, L-T," the voice of MM/2 Kleinfelder replied in his ear. "Not a thing."

"All right. You and Franklin, pack it in. We're aborting."

He raised an LI scope to his eyes and scanned the hacienda grounds. The sentries were continuing their rounds as though nothing had happened. But there could be a patrol out in the jungle somewhere.

"Okay," Esposito said, nervously fingering the CAR-15 carbine he was carrying. He seemed to be trying to make up his mind. "Okay. We'll have to abort. Can we make it back to where they dropped you this morning?"

Drake shook his head. "In about five minutes, this mountain is going to be crawling with bad guys. We'll call for a dust-off at an alternate LZ. What about your man down there?"

Esposito shook his head. "There's nothing we can do for him now."

He didn't like it, but Drake had to admit that the DEA agent was right on that one.

And the longer they squatted here at the OP, the more likely it was that they'd be found. "Right. Timmons, pack the sat gear. Ski, secure the camera. Time to *di di mau.*"

Fifteen minutes later, the SEALs were making their way up the northern face of the mountain. There was no sign of pursuit, but Drake knew they were being followed. The blackness of the jungle had turned malevolent, hostile.

"Pull up," he said. They had enough of a head start by now to call a brief halt. "Radio. Rest of you, perimeter defense."

Franklin was humping the team's PRC-41 radio in a rucksack frame. Weighing forty pounds, the Prick 41 was an ideal radio for ground-to-air communications. Its range was restricted to line of sight, but Drake knew that a Navy E-2C Hawkeye was orbiting somewhere off the coast, waiting to relay a pickup call like this one to a ready JSOC helicopter.

He set the radio to the emergency frequency. "Mosquito, Mosquito, this is Peeping Tom." Mosquito was the helo's call sign. "Come in, Mosquito."

"Peeping Tom, this here's Mosquito," a voice replied with a warm accent that sounded like deep Texas. "Go ahead."

"Mosquito, Peeping Tom. Bad skiing on the slopes.

Request immediate ski lift. Site Delta Green, repeat, Delta Green."

"That's a big roger, son," the voice replied. "Ski lift at Delta Green. We're on the way. ETA sixty mikes."

One hour. The team should reach the alternate LZ in forty minutes. "Copy, Mosquito. We'll be waiting with the welcome mat! Tom out!"

Drake replaced the radio handset in Franklin's pack. "Move out!"

The team set a rapid pace up and over the hill. The alternate landing zone lay beyond the first ridge, dangerously close to the OP site, but amid terrain so rugged that a Special Ops helo, skimming in just above the sea, should have little trouble avoiding the rather inefficient Colombian radar. Satellite photos showed a clearing large enough for the chopper to set down for an emergency dust-off. It would be hairy navigating the mountains by night, but the pilot would be wearing infrared gear that would turn night to day for him.

All of them were breathing hard when they reached the clearing three-quarters of an hour later. Esposito had made the last few hundred meters supported between Timmons and Kleinfelder. He was gasping for breath as he sank to a log at the clearing's edge, gulping air. "How . . . long . . . ?"

Drake realized he was breathing hard, too. Damn. Ten weeks with Project RAMROD and his body had lost some of its physical edge. He lifted the Velcro strap shielding his luminous watch dial. "Fifteen minutes. Kleinfelder. Timmons. Check it out."

The two SEALs vanished silently into the darkness. Minutes later they reappeared. "Clear," Kleinfelder

14 *Robert Cain*

said. "Looks like an old hurricane blowdown. Still no sign of the bad guys."

"I think we gave 'em the slip," Franklin added.

"Okay. Ski, you and Timmons set out the lights. Franklin, gimme the radio." He thought he could make out the far-off, drumming thutter of an approaching helicopter. Pray God it was the right one. . . .

As Kaminski and Timmons began placing battery-powered torches in the clearing, Drake opened the tactical frequency again. "Mosquito, this is Peeping Tom. Come in, Mosquito. We hear you in the area. Over."

"Copy, Tom," the Texan voice replied. "We're comin' up on the LZ. Let's see your ID, boy."

"Show him the colors, Kleinfelder."

The SEAL pulled a flashlight from his rucksack and shone it into the sky. The lens was covered with a red filter.

"Peeping Tom, Mosquito. I see a red light."

"Roger that, Mosquito. Red light. LZ is clear. Come on in."

The landing-zone beacons, six of them spaced ten paces apart in a large T, cast their beams into the sky toward the north at a forty-five-degree angle, providing a landing target for the chopper. Seconds later, a shape materialized out of the dark sky, belly-lit by the LZ lights.

It was an old Huey Slick, painted in faded jungle camo colors, the cargo door open. There were no insignia or other markings, not even hull numbers. The Huey drifted downward until it was within a few feet of the ground, drowning every sound with the thunderous *whup-whup-whup* of its rotors. Palm fronds, branches, and ferns whipped and lashed around the crouching SEALs, and bits of gravel stung Drake's face. A spotlight snapped on from the helo's cargo deck.

"Let's haul ass, guys," the Texan said over the radio. "I'm double-parked here."

"Go!" Esposito yelled. "Move! Move! Move!"

Esposito was already well into the clearing, loping toward the hovering Slick, one hand clutching his boonie hat to his head as he crouched low beneath the rotors.

Shit! Since when had the DEA guy been leading this op? "Esposito! Hold it!"

Too late. Timmons was running after Esposito toward the helo, followed by Kleinfelder and Franklin.

Warning shrieked in Drake's brain. Something was *wrong.* Shadows moved on the Huey's cargo deck, behind the blinding light. Soldiers were dropping from the hovering aircraft, fanning out across the field. . . .

"Ambush!" Drake yelled, throwing himself to the ground. He groped for his Uzi. "Down!"

But the others could not hear him over the rotor noise.

Franklin staggered in front of him, then dropped to the ground, dark wet patches staining the back of his fatigues. A few meters ahead, Kleinfelder flipped backward out of the glare of the searchlight as though struck by a sledgehammer.

He heard the stuttering bark of a machine gun. Someone was hosing the SEALs from the chopper's cargo deck with an M-60, sweeping back and forth as the Huey rose above the field. Kaminski was down . . .

and Timmons. Damn it, his men were dying, dying before they knew what was happening!

A line of armed men was advancing now across the field, backlit by the searchlight. Drake saw one gunman stop, raise the unmistakable silhouette of an M-16, and fire a deliberate burst into the dark, twisted shape sprawled at his feet.

Drake knew he couldn't stay here, and if he opened fire he'd be cut down like the rest. He hadn't been seen yet, but he was willing to bet that the ambushers knew exactly how many men were in the SEAL team. They'd come looking for him.

The Prick 41 lay close by, where Franklin had dropped it. Timing his movement to the sweep of the searchlight, he rolled across the ground, snagged one of the radio's carrying straps, then rose and bolted for the jungle.

He'd been seen! Wood splintered from a tree trunk beside his head as he dodged into the forest. Behind him, the helicopter lifted higher above the clearing, the M-60 doorgunner reaching out after him with bursts of hot lead. Infrared, he thought as he ran. The pilot can see in the dark. . . .

Drake kept running, alone now as he'd never been alone before in his life.

⬤ Chapter Two

"So then I E&E'd," Drake said. He shifted in his chair. It seemed strange, sitting in an office again. This was the second time in twenty-four hours that he'd told his story, but it had lost none of its immediacy for him. He still felt the horror of the ambush, the wet and mud and heat of the jungle. "Took two days to reach Palomino, about twenty klicks east of the Salazar place."

"Was there any sign of pursuit?" James Weston wanted to know. The distinguished-looking, gray-haired director of Project RAMROD was making notes on a pad in front of him. "Any mobilization at all by the people at the hacienda?"

"None that I was aware of, sir."

The third man in the room was also taking notes. "And you're certain, Lieutenant, that the helicopter was not Colombian military." Brigadier General Maxwell Sinclair was the number-three man in the U.S. Joint Special Operations Command, and as such, Drake's commanding officer.

"Yes, sir," Drake replied. "I saw a mix of weapons, uniforms, stuff like that. Mercenaries would be my guess. Paramilitary, certainly. The pilot . . . well, I never got a look at him, but on the radio he sure as hell *sounded* American. Texan, I think." He looked at Weston. "You looked into who was supposed to fly the dust-off, of course."

"First thing we checked," Weston said. "The scheduled pilot was Michael Howard Braden. CIA contract man. He's flown helos for the Company before." Weston paused and gave an ironic smile. "And he *is* from Texas. But the records show that Braden took sick just before the mission. Dysentery. Checked into Gorgas Army Hospital, Panama."

"His replacement?" General Sinclair asked.

"We don't know. He was replaced . . . but there are no records on whoever took the run." Weston shrugged. "Sometimes these CIA contract operations leave something to be desired in their . . . accountability." He fixed his stare on Drake once more. "So what happened then? You said you reached Palomino."

"Yes, sir. I found a sloop, a native fishing boat, pulled up on the sand. Nobody was around, so I appropriated her, hoisted sail, and headed north. Once I was out of sight of land, I used the Prick 41 to raise a Coast Guard E-2C over the southern Caribbean. An hour later, I was picked up by a Sea King and taken to the *Decisive*. That's a Coast Guard cutter pulling drug-interdiction duty just outside Colombia's twelve-mile limit. Twenty-four hours later I was at Fort Gulik." He spread his hands. "And today I'm here."

"Very resourceful," Sinclair said thoughtfully. "An excellent job all around."

"It would have been better if I hadn't lost my team," Drake said bitterly.

"I see nothing that you could have done differently, son."

"It's not the sort of thing you can just walk away from, General." The disaster in Colombia had been weighing on Drake ever since he'd eluded the ambush. He didn't know what else he *could* have done . . . but the responsibility had been his.

"You've got to, Lieutenant. What happened, well . . ." Sinclair's mouth twisted unpleasantly. "It's obvious now that we have a leak. A bad one. You couldn't help that."

Weston consulted his notes. "Where do you think the leak is, General? The DEA?"

"Possible," Sinclair replied. The two men began a low, rapid-fire exchange, comparing the notes they'd taken during Drake's debriefing.

Drake looked away, gazing out the large window in one wall of Weston's office. There was little to see: the flat, scrub-brush brown of Peninsula marshland, and in the distance the metallic-gray brightness of the York River beneath the dull overcast of an early-fall day.

Camp Peary, the CIA's training center and operations facility a few miles north of Williamsburg, Virginia, was a far cry from the mountains and jungles of Colombia. Called "the Farm" by initiates, it was disguised as a Pentagon research-and-testing center, with 480 wooded acres concealing obstacle courses, weapons ranges, a complete Eastern European border town, and training grounds. It *also* housed genuine research-and-testing facilities, the better to maintain the camp's cover.

RAMROD was one of them.

RAMROD's headquarters resided in a nondescript government building supposedly devoted to agricultural studies. The reality, as might be expected in such an environment, was quite different.

Drake was suddenly aware that someone had asked him a question. "I beg your pardon, sir?"

"I asked if you felt up to a PARET run this afternoon," Weston said. "We have some Group Seven VIPs coming in this afternoon, and they've been promised a show."

"No problem, Mr. Weston," Drake replied. "I feel fine."

"You're sure? We can always grab another guinea pig somewhere."

"Hey, after three days in the jungle, I don't think CORA can hit me with anything I can't handle."

"Good enough." Weston stood behind his desk. "Gentlemen, let's go downstairs."

They left the director's third-floor office, passing through a secretarial suite and into the elevator foyer outside.

Stepping into a waiting elevator, Weston produced an ID card from his wallet and slipped the magnetic strip embedded in one end into a nondescript slot in the control panel next to the floor-selection buttons. Dragging the card sharply through the slot, he then pressed the red "emergency stop" button. The door closed and the elevator started to descend.

The panel showed stops for three floors and a basement, but the elevator car dropped past the parking level, still descending. When the doors opened a moment later, they stepped into a reception area brilliantly lit by fluorescent lights. On the tile floor was a large mosaic—Leonardo's famous engraving illustrating the geometric perfection in the proportions of the human body. Beneath the feet, spelled out in capitals, was a single word: RAMROD.

They were not challenged, but Drake felt the eyes of several OS men on them as they crossed the logo to the security desk. OS—the CIA's Office of Security—provided RAMROD's guards, tight-lipped men in black uniforms and helmets and armed with M-16s. "SECURITY" was written across the white strips on their helmets and on their MP-style armbands.

Weston signed in, then registered his palm print on a reader at the desk. Sinclair did the same, followed by Drake. Special authorization was required for Sinclair. While the general had the appropriate security clearance, he was not a member of RAMROD and his credentials were given special scrutiny. Each of them was given an ID pass to be pinned to his lapel and warned—as always—that he must wear the pass at all times while in RAMROD's secure areas.

Security was taken very seriously in Project RAMROD's lower levels.

Walking quickly now down echoing tile corridors, the three men followed a red line on the floor, though they'd all come this way many times before. The hallways were bustling with men and women, all tagged with security IDs, coming and going about their business. Project RAMROD's workers included military personnel like Drake, CIA people like Weston and the OS guards, men and women from Rand Corporation, DARPA, IBM, employees from a dozen other government-sponsored think tanks and corporations across the country.

They reached a set of sealed doors beneath a sign reading LAB ONE: CLEAN ACCESS. They showed their passes to a pair of OS men with M-16s, then Weston ran his magnetic card through a reader on the wall. The doors slid open and they walked into the gowning room.

The far end of the room was a double glass wall, looking into a high-tech electronics lab. From lockers at the side Drake and the others removed knee-length white smocks, disposable paper shower caps, and booties. The RAMROD logo was repeated on their smocks, which they donned over their regular clothing. Lab One maintained a clean room environment, and the several dozen men and women moving among the gleaming consoles and computer terminals on the other side of the glass wall were all similarly attired. When they were ready, Weston used his magnetic access card a final time, and the three of them stepped into the shining spotlessness of RAMROD's main lab.

As always, Drake was struck by the lab's similarities to a hospital operating room—the lights, the cleanliness, the air of purposeful activity among the white-gowned attendants. The center of attention was the figure of a nude human male spread-eagled on a stainless-steel table. Despite the OR atmosphere, the subject looked more like a torture victim than a surgical patient.

The subject was called Rod, and he—*it*, rather—was not human.

RAMROD. It was a typically contrived government acronym that did more to mask the project's purpose than explain it. The name was short for *R*and *A*rtificially intelligent *M*ilitary *RO*botic *D*evice, an unwieldy title further shortened by the men and women who worked on him to Rod. RAMROD's centerpiece, the reason for the project's existence, was a humanoid robot originally designed as an all-purpose military weapon with the strength, speed, and endurance of a machine, but with the flexibility, the *adaptability* of a man.

RAMROD had been conceived in the early seventies as a joint R&D project by Rand and DARPA, with the goal of creating a combat robot. That had been during the final years of Vietnam, when some of the higher-ranking ponderers at the Pentagon had begun looking at alternatives to the use of half-trained, teenage draftees in combat.

Designed to function in any environment, to use any weapon, to exhibit literally inhuman patience, strength, endurance, stealth, and speed, a few robotic soldiers might replace whole regiments of eighteen-year-olds. Why send in platoon after platoon of teenagers to take some fortified, blood-drenched hill in the jungle, it was reasoned, when a single squad of RAMRODs, air-dropped in full Combat Mod, could infiltrate and destroy the target before the enemy even realized he was under attack?

Though RAMROD had produced limited test prototypes by the early eighties, the DOD budget for the program had been canceled in 1984. At a unit cost of upward of two billion dollars, not even the Pentagon could afford a very large army of robot soldiers.

But the fall of the budgetary ax had not ended the

project. Supporters of the program, arguing that RAM-
ROD represented incredible strides in the fields of artificial intelligence and robotics, had pointed out that
with billions already spent in R&D, a few million more
to create a fully operational prototype that could be
field-evaluated would not break the bank. There were
other uses to which true artificial intelligence would be
put one day—exploring space or the bottom of the sea,
working in deadly environments in factories or nuclear
power plants, serving in law enforcement or firefighter
roles . . . the possibilities were endless.

So RAMROD had continued, funded now through
the CIA's Directorate of Science and Technology. The
Central Intelligence Agency had been in on RAMROD
since the beginning, the project facilities had been constructed on the Company's Camp Peary reserve for security purposes, and it was only natural that a CIA
executive head up the whole program.

That was James Weston's role. It was interesting,
Drake thought, how the room grew silent as soon as
Weston walked through the sliding glass doors and
onto the lab floor.

"Carry on, people," Weston announced. "Don't
mind us."

A slim, attractive woman, her long blond hair hidden
by her cap, looked up from the surgical table. "We
never do, Mr. Weston," Dr. Heather McDaniels said.
She grinned at Drake. "Hello, Chris. Welcome back!
How was your . . . vacation?"

When he'd been pulled out of RAMROD and given
TAD—temporary attached duty—orders to join the
SNOWDROP op into Colombia, the story passed around

the RAMROD lab was that he was vacationing in Florida. No one believed it for a moment, of course.

"Didn't even have time to get a suntan," Drake replied. "Say! Your friend here's looking almost human."

It was a running joke among RAMROD team personnel. Rod had been looking "almost human" for two months now, ever since they'd begun molding the soft synthetic that served as the robot's skin to simulate wrinkles, blemishes, moles, and the minor imperfections of detail that had transformed him from a department-store mannequin into something that, dressed and walking, would be indistinguishable from a human.

Biomimicry, they called it. An android, a robot designed to look like a man. Rod had begun his—was *life* the right word?—his existence, anyway, as a Tinkertoy construct of titanium-steel alloy and camera eyes.

Now, lying stretched out on the table, Rod appeared to be perfectly human, a man in his mid-thirties, lean and hard-muscled, with wavy, light brown hair that was almost blond and features that Drake had once heard described as "ruggedly handsome." Upright, the robot stood three inches taller than Drake's compact five-foot-nine-inch frame, but he had a lighter build. That lightness was illusory, of course. A guess-your-weight barker at a carnival might have set Rod's weight at 170 pounds. In fact, in its current configuration, the RAMROD robot would have tipped the scales at 290.

The skin looked and felt lifelike, radiating a body temperature of thirty-seven degrees Celsius. Special programming imitated respiration and, at need, could mimic heartbeat and pulse. Extraordinary effort had been expended on such added niceties as wrinkles around the eyes, moles, eyelashes, body hair, and entirely gratuitous nipples, genitals, and navel. The idea, as the updated RAMROD project directives had succinctly phrased it, was "to simulate in detail external aspects of human appearance, such that reasonably severe inspection, including strip searches or exposure in public locker rooms or lavatories, will not reveal the artificial nature of the subject."

Most of the Rand and DARPA technicians assumed that the CIA wanted the realism so it could employ Rod as a robot spy. Never mind the fact that Rod would never have made it past an airport metal detector.

Drake leaned closer. "Hello, Rod."

"Can't hear you," a technician said. "He's off-line."

"Sack time, huh?" Drake saw that the robot's right shoulder had been opened up for some mechanical adjustment, the skin peeled back and held by clamps, a steel access panel underneath removed. The SEAL was used to the sight by now, though he still felt a small shock each time he looked into the robot's interior, expecting, perhaps, to see blood and bone.

Instead, uncountable slender, colored wires arranged in compact bundles shared the cavity with multiple layers of intricate, needle-slim parts that seemed to slide across one another with frictionless ease as a technician manipulated them with a probe.

Dr. Edward Costrini was watching the manipulations through a binocular viewer positioned over the opening. On a TV monitor behind his head, the complexity of the robot's servohydraulic system flexed and rippled like living muscle tissue.

"So," Drake said cheerfully. "Problem with this pile of spare parts?"

"Problem?" Costrini mimicked. The deputy head of the assembly team lifted his head from the viewer eyepieces. "What problem? I *like* testing three hundred separate solenoid relays looking for the one that's stuck. It gives my life such *meaning*, such *purpose*. . . ."

Dr. McDaniels grinned. "Don't mind Ted," she said. "He got up on the wrong side of his oil change this morning."

There was a long-standing rivalry between RAM-ROD's mechanical engineers and the computer people, the clackers and the hackers as they called themselves. "Do I detect a note of hostility on the assembly team?" Weston asked.

"Not at all," Costrini said. "Dr. McDaniels simply refuses to believe that her programming could possibly be at fault. Always it's an *assembly* problem, never the programming."

"We hear replays of this argument all the time," Weston explained to General Sinclair. "Last week it was whether the reason the robot couldn't blink was a programming glitch or something mechanical."

"We never did figure out that one," McDaniels said.

"Certainly we did. It was programming. As usual."

"We corrected the programming and he *still* can't blink." She looked at a clock on the wall. "We're ready for the feed anytime, Mr. Weston. And we can give you a unit demo as soon as Ted finds the trouble."

"Unless, of course, what we're dealing with is a program glitch. In that case we'll be lucky if we can go on-line by . . . *shit!*"

"Whatcha got?" McDaniels turned and studied the monitor screen. Blunt-tipped probes, hundreds of times larger than life, slid beneath hair-thin wires that grew like thick-clumped forest trees on the screen.

"Defective solenoid relay. It's not drawing power at all."

McDaniels grinned. "Mechanical. I rest my case. That's five you owe me, Ted."

"You'll get it payday. Fred, let's have another R-30 solenoid here. Make it a different batch number, huh? I think we'll have to ditch the one-fifty-eights. This is the third time this has happened."

There was a feedback squeal from a loudspeaker on the lab wall. "Attention, Mr. Weston. Attention, Mr. Weston. Your party is waiting for you at the security desk."

"Time to go." Weston looked at Drake. "Lieutenant, take it easy. This is only a demo PARET run."

"No sweat, Mr. Weston. Like I said, this is a vacation after my . . . uh . . . *vacation.*"

"We'll be watching from here. Have fun."

Walking through separate doors, they left the assembly team and the inert patient on the table. In the gowning room, Drake shed his smock, booties, and cap, then found his combat blacks in the locker where he'd left them a week before. After pinning his security pass to his turtleneck top, he took a side door, ducked into a stairwell, and headed down two levels.

His destination was the building's armory.

It was a very bad part of town.

The man got out of a white C&P phone-company van. "This shouldn't take long."

"Right, Luis," the blond-haired man in the passenger seat said. "Don't get mugged."

The area was primarily Hispanic, a Latino enclave in southern Virginia Beach, a blending of Puerto Rican and Mexican elements. Barrio music boomed from a ghetto blaster on the sidewalk. Voices called to one another in Spanish. Graffiti on the walls proclaimed that this was the territory of *Los Salvajes*, the Savages.

He didn't have far to walk. Three-story buildings rose on all sides, ugly, far-decayed monstrosities packed four to a city block, their walls covered with graffiti, the alleyways between them cluttered with garbage. On the street corner, several Latino-looking youths were doing business. Cars would pull up at the curb, there would be a short conversation with the occupants, and then small plastic bags were exchanged for money. The block's protector, an ugly, mustached tough in sunglasses, lounged against the crumbling facade of a liquor store, narrowly watching Luis.

In an alleyway, Luis stepped up to a wooden door and knocked, then stepped back so the occupants could see through the fish-eye lens in the peephole that he was alone. There was a rattling of locks, and then the door opened. A swarthy face peered at him.

"Qué tal, Julio?" Luis asked.

"Quien es?" another voice demanded from the gloom. Luis heard the snick of an automatic weapon's bolt being drawn.

"Fresco, Chaco," Julio called back over his shoulder. "It's the *man.* C'mon in."

Luis masked his distaste as he stepped inside. The mingled stenches of alcohol and garbage, of vomit, urine, and feces, were overpowering. In the kitchen, a man and a gaunt-looking woman bent over the stove, where something simmered in a pot. A box of baking soda rested on the counter beside them; neatly wrapped packets of aluminum foil were lined up on the kitchen table.

He heard a baby crying upstairs.

The apartment building was headquarters for the local chapter of *Los Salvajes,* a Hispanic gang that dealt in crack cocaine in cities up and down the East Coast. Luis did not like dealing with these people directly, but Diamond's orders had been explicit . . . and urgent. Luis would have to recruit the necessary people himself, to ensure that there were no screw-ups.

Chaco loomed up out of the shadows. "Don't often see you around these parts, man. Whatcha want?"

"I got a job for you," Luis replied. "I need four guys. Today."

"Cuanto?"

"One K apiece now. Five more afterward."

Julio whistled. "I'll take a piece of that. What's the job?"

Luis smiled. "Don't worry, man. You'll love it."

He'd used the Savages for errands before. So long as the job was simple, brutal, and direct, they'd have no problems carrying out their orders.

Luis began explaining what he needed.

⟨ᴡ⟩ Chapter Three

THE WOMAN STEPPED OUT suddenly from behind the corner of a building a few yards in front of Drake. She was tall, blond, and dressed to kill, with dangling earrings and an expensive-looking red dress. The light from a sodium-vapor street lamp on a nearby corner gave the leather of her pocketbook a metallic gleam. . . .

Drake dropped into a crouch, the heavy .45 automatic already swinging up in a two-handed aim when his brain registered the fact that the woman was no threat. He let the motion continue, raising the barrel until it was aimed at the ceiling.

The woman took no notice of Drake but stopped on the curb next to an Infiniti sports coupe and began fumbling in the pocketbook for her car keys.

In one smooth motion Drake touched the release stud, and the magazine, down to two rounds now, slid from the pistol's grip and clattered at his feet. His left hand slipped a fresh magazine into the .45 and snicked it home. That gave him eight rounds, seven in the mag and one up the spout.

The woman continued to ignore him, unlocking her car door.

The man who leaped out behind her looked like a typical street tough, a gang logo on his motorcycle jacket, his leering grin exposing yellow and uneven teeth. The Walther PPK was already pressed against the girl's head, his left arm pinning her body against his chest.

The woman screamed as Drake snapped the .45 into line with the mugger's face. "She's dead!" the thug yelled, his mouth close behind her ear, but the words were chopped off by the detonation of Drake's pistol. He fired once . . . twice, deafening explosions coupled to the appearance of twin red spots side by side on the mugger's forehead like an extra pair of eyes.

Noise, movement . . . or some combat-honed sixth sense dragged Drake forward, down and around, facing right. A man burst from a doorway on the front step of a brownstone apartment. A few feet away, another woman, this one standing behind a baby carriage, yelled and pointed. The man held a Smith & Wesson revolver in his right hand . . .

. . . and wore a police officer's uniform. Drake followed his new target only long enough to verify that the cop wasn't aiming at him, then swung his weapon to cover the woman. She was pulling something long and black from the baby buggy, snapping the pump action, bringing the shotgun to bear on Drake's chest.

He continued his down-and-forward movement, taking the fall on his shoulder and rolling with it. His shot was not aimed—there was no *time* to aim—but he squeezed off shot after shot as the woman squeezed the trigger of her sawed-off Mossberg M500. The shotgun's deafening roar obliterated the bark of the .45 auto as

Drake rolled across the ground, firing now rightside up, now upside down as he dragged his aim down toward the woman's center of mass. Red spots tracked down the brownstone's wall as he fired, one-two-three-four. The fifth round hit her left shoulder, the sixth high in her chest.

Slowly, Drake rose to his feet. His .45's slide was locked back, the magazine empty. He took a deep breath and tasted the tiny, biting stink of cordite. The range lighting came on overhead. The images on the target screens were still there, but dimmer in the bright light than they had been, less substantial, less realistic. The woman with the shotgun still glared at him over the ballooning muzzle flash of her weapon, while behind him, the mugger held his PPK against the screaming woman's head, their images frozen in time.

"Drake, Christopher C.," a quiet voice said from a hidden speaker somewhere overhead. "Run number three-five-nine complete. Time two minutes fifty-six seconds. Score ninety-four percent. No collateral damage."

Civilians, Drake thought. "Collateral damage" meant civilians . . . innocent bystanders.

Damn, but the simulation was realistic! He took several more deep breaths, willing the racing of his heart to slow, then stood up. It was like this after every run. The techies who had wired him up must be having a field day with his vital signs right now.

The FBI had the training simulator they called the Fun House at Quantico, while down at Fort Bragg, Delta, and the other Special Operations Command units routinely ran through the four-room target gallery they called the House of Horrors. Drake had been through both courses frequently with SEAL Team Eight. Twice, during cross-training assignments overseas, he'd even been through the notorious Killing House used by Britain's SAS.

At RAMROD, the personal combat simulations unit was called Kiddie Land. Instead of the pop-up cardboard targets once employed, huge projection screens twenty feet tall displayed the life-size videotaped images of actors going about their business on a typical city street. Multiple screens could be arranged in various ways, allowing a trainee to stroll through Kiddie Land's city streets or the interiors of buildings.

The trick was *not* to fire at the citizens engaged in activities that were legitimate, if occasionally startling or unexpected, but to kill the thugs, gunmen, assassins, terrorists, and gun-wielding crazies who appeared at random, in varying degrees of light and cover, and in attacks that were never the same twice. Each shot, registered by embedded sensors that detected the impact of the low-velocity plastic pellets, was recorded by CORA, the computer handling the simulation, and graded according to its likelihood of killing or disabling the target. A kill froze the image, hopefully before it had "fired," while the hit was marked by a low-energy laser.

His face bathed with sweat, Drake released the slide and holstered the weapon. With both hands then, he reached up and unhooked his chin strap. The helmet he was wearing was cumbersome. He lifted it off over his head, careful not to pull free the cables that plugged into receptacles in the back. A wisp of cold vapor, re-

leased from the superconductor refrigerant pack, boiled
away in the air.

Greg Irvin and several Rand technicians walked toward him. "Nice run, Lieutenant," Irvin said.

"Thanks." Drake handed the helmet to a techie.
"What's the bad news? Did Miss Mossberg there kill
me?"

"Almost but no cigar," Irvin said. He looked down
at his clipboard. "CORA says . . . thirty-two-percent
chance that you were disabled. You got her either way,
whether she hit you or not. That was pretty fancy shoot-
ing!"

"Pretty fancy panic, you mean," Drake replied. He
jerked a thumb at the mugger still leering from behind
the woman in the red dress. Drake's two shots had
missed the woman's head by less than the span of a
man's hand. "That HR bit was cute."

"Glad you liked it. Maybe next time you can try it
full auto."

Drake laughed. "Full-auto head shots are strictly
Hollywood, Irv! And I'd better not catch you telling
CORA any different! I—"

"Lieutenant Drake?" An amplified voice boomed
over Kiddie Land's PA system. "Knock off for a while.
Come on back to Lab One."

"The Master summons," Irvin said, grinning.

"Yeah. Guess I'll catch you later." He started back
toward the armory to check in his pistol.

In 1986, President Reagan announced the formation
of several multidepartmental task forces charged with
battling the rapidly worsening scourge of illegal drugs

entering the United States. Most of these groups—involved in fighting the war on drugs through education, better law enforcement, stricter laws—were overt, and matters of public record. A few, however, were covert.

Group Seven was one of these, a secret government task force with members drawn from each of the bureaucracies already involved in the war on drugs. Its personnel included members of the Drug Enforcement Administration, the FBI, the CIA, the State Department, and the military; its chairman was Frank Buchanan, the Democratic senator from Florida already well-known for his outspoken advocacy of using the military to track down the drug barons, the *narcotraficantes* who were flooding America with their poisons, and bring them to the United States for trial.

Rumor had it that more than one attempt had already been made on the senator's life.

The situation was out of control, and growing worse. America's cities were crumbling into drug-soaked pits of crime, despair, and violence. More than one major police force had been rocked by scandal within the past few years, with allegations of corruption, payoffs from drug lords, even narcotics trafficking by policemen. The mayor of Washington, D.C., had been convicted on a cocaine charge, and the leaders of several other cities were under Federal investigation as well. The Border Patrol, Customs, and DEA agents trying to stem the flood of cocaine and heroin across America's borders and through her ports were being overwhelmed by an enemy more numerous, better-armed, better-paid, and far more vicious than they.

Group Seven was searching for a way to fight back before it was too late.

And James Weston was convinced that RAMROD might be the weapon they needed. A combat robot, originally developed to military specifications, could do things no *human* narcotics agent could imagine.

"It's a whole new way of programming computers," Weston said. He was standing in Lab One, addressing four men and two women who were, like him, members of Group Seven. "PARET lets Rod duplicate the way humans think . . . lets him *reason.*"

They had just watched Drake's simulation run on a large TV monitor on the lab wall. Roger Menefee shook his head. "James, are you going to stand there and tell us that that gadget your man wore on his head somehow recorded his ability with a gun? That you can transfer that ability to . . ." He gestured lamely toward the table in the middle of the lab, where McDaniels and the other RAMROD assembly personnel were monitoring the simulator results. "That *thing* over there?"

Weston smiled. Roger Menefee was Group Seven's liaison with the Drug Enforcement Administration. As an agent he'd led the team that bagged eighty pounds of heroin at O'Hare International in Chicago eight years earlier. As a DEA deputy regional director, he'd coordinated a massive search-and-seizure operation in Arizona in 1989, discovering a half-mile tunnel beneath the Mexican border, a tunnel that had been the entry path for thousands of pounds of cocaine in the past several years. He was a good man and a sharp one, but he had never been keen on the idea of incorporating RAMROD into Group Seven's antinarcotics efforts.

"That's exactly what I'm saying, Roger."

"Rod is more than a robot, Mr. Menefee," Dr. Theodore Godiesky added, coming to Weston's aid. RAMROD's technical liaison with the CIA was a small, athletic man in his fifties with sparse, sandy hair and glasses that looked too large for his narrow face. Godiesky had been with the CIA's Science and Technology Directorate until, like Weston, he'd been loaned to RAMROD. He'd been with the project for four years now but had only recently been recruited for Group Seven.

"RAMROD demonstrates true artificial intelligence," Godiesky continued. "Or 'AI' as the computer jocks like to say. It goes far beyond any traditional programming method. In a sense, the system we're developing programs itself from moment to moment."

Senator Buchanan chuckled. "You don't mean that it really thinks for itself, do you?"

"Depends on how you define thinking," Godiesky said. "Some of us are still debating that one."

"Come on over here," Weston said. He led the way toward the table. The technicians stepped aside so the visitors could have a closer look. Rod was no longer nude but was wearing black trousers and combat boots. His chest was still bare, however, so that the techs could get at his opened right side. A heavy cable ran up onto the table and into what appeared to be an I/O port recessed into the machine's body. "Rod here represents advances in computer technology that are ten, maybe twenty years ahead of anything else in the world."

Barbara Roberts peered into the opening. She was

Seven's FBI liaison and was also an expert in programming. "Feeding time?" she asked. "What's he eat—AC or DC?"

"Rod has his own on-board power source," Weston said. "Lightweight superconductor batteries that give him about three days of power for normal operations, less if he has to exert himself. No, that cable's his PARET feed. He's busily digesting Lieutenant Drake's last run through Kiddie Land."

PARET: *PA*ttern *RE*plication and *T*ransfer. That, Weston knew, was arguably RAMROD's single greatest technological triumph, the breakthrough that had made true AI a working reality.

Early in RAMROD, when it was still a Department of Defense project, it had been realized that no computer, however complex, could duplicate the processes of the human mind through traditional line-by-line programming. As Weston was fond of explaining to anyone who would listen, a simple action that adult humans took for granted—climbing stairs, for instance—could require literally thousands upon thousands of lines of programming code. Just getting the computer to recognize stairs as stairs through its camera eyes was a major victory, and there were endless variables of height, grade, and texture to the steps; of possible motions; of balance; of *decisions* to be made from instant to instant, such as which running programs to suspend when attitude sensors reported that balance had been lost.

RAMROD's engineers could have spent billions of dollars simply developing a machine able to climb stairs and do nothing else.

Yet they were trying to develop a robot that could

climb stairs or leap from a helicopter, seek cover in the woods or wade through a swamp, load a rifle or throw a hand grenade, recognize friends or shoot an enemy, use a parachute or pilot a combat aircraft. The point of building a true android robot was that it would be able to do anything a man could do. To program each task separately would have been worse than a nightmare. It would have been impossible.

"RAMROD has been teaching us a lot about how the human mind and body work," Costrini explained. "For example, his muscular actions are carried out by hydraulic pistons, thousands of them, duplicating the actions of human muscle fibers. Each pump is controlled by its own microprocessor chip—a computer, if you will—about the size of the head of a pin. There are over a million chips in Rod's body, connected in parallel to his central autonomic processor and its backup. With the whole system working in concert, with appropriate training, Rod here can display any range of motion or activity possible to a human . . . and then some."

"And this is how we train him," Dr. McDaniels added, picking up one of the heavy, ceramic-armored headpieces from a nearby table. "A PARET helmet. We call it the thinking cap. When you engage in some activity—climbing stairs, loading a gun, whatever—the neurons in your brain fire in a specific pattern. If you wear a PARET helmet, CORA can read those patterns and translate them into a form Rod can store and use. Rod's primary computer duplicates human neural networking."

"Excuse me," Tricia Ashby said. She was a State Department expert in Latin American affairs, recruited into Group Seven for her expertise in the drug problem. " 'CORA'?"

"That's the AI expert system that runs simulations like the one you saw a few minutes ago and oversees the robot's training."

"What's CORA stand for?" Barbara Roberts wanted to know.

"Computer Optimization of Referent Analogues," Dr. Godiesky explained. "A fancy way of saying she directs the patterning process—what we call 'referent analogues'—in Rod's brain. She reads the robot's mind, if you will. . . ."

"She reads Rod's *soul*," McDaniels added. "And writes on it. She's what we use to teach Rod here how to be human."

Menefee snorted. "Interesting concept. A computer with a soul."

"It's incredible," Senator Buchanan said softly.

The double glass doors at the end of the lab slid open, and Lieutenant Drake walked in, still buttoning his smock over his combat blacks.

"Chris!" Weston said, grateful for an opportunity to steer the conversation away from the metaphysical. "Let me introduce you to some people. Dr. Godiesky, General Sinclair you know, of course. This is Senator Buchanan . . . Barb Roberts . . . Tricia Ashby . . . Roger Menefee. Ladies, gentlemen, this is Lieutenant Christopher Drake, our resident tame SEAL."

"Nice to meet you, son," Buchanan said. "That was an impressive performance."

"Thank you, Senator," Drake replied, shaking his hand.

"Indeed," Menefee added. "I had no idea our SEALs were such . . . gunslingers."

"SEAL Eight is always training for hostage situations, sir. They teach us to shoot in just about any situation or position you could imagine."

"Which is why you were chosen for this project," Tricia Ashby put in. "Fast reflexes, quick thinking, that sort of thing?"

"I suppose so." He glanced down at himself, plucking the smock away from sweat-soaked blacks. "I doubt it was because I'm such a flashy dresser."

That raised a chuckle.

"Dr. McDaniels," Weston said, "was telling us about PARETing."

"The important thing to remember," she said, "is that PARET allows Rod's programming to function much the way ours does. What a human can learn to do, so can Rod . . . but much, much faster. He can react to his environment like a human, only faster. He can *think* like a human, only faster. He actually programs himself as he goes along, learning from experience. He has a built-in data-acquisition routine that can only be described as 'curiosity.' He—"

"Good God, Miss McDaniels," Menefee interrupted. "Are you saying this . . . this *thing* actually thinks for itself? That it's . . . it's . . . ."

"I believe the concept you are searching for is 'self-aware,' " the robot said. The newcomers around the table jumped in unison, as if they'd been given an electric shock. "And yes," Rod added. *"I think I am."*

Amid a low babble of nervous comments and surprise, Costrini released a lock under the table, then swiveled the top up until Rod was almost upright, still disconcertingly stretched out by his bonds. The head moved—there was just a hint of unnatural stiffness there, Weston thought—turning cold, steel-gray eyes on Menefee.

"I gather from your records that you are Roger Dean Menefee," Rod said. The voice was smooth, low-pitched, and natural, not electronic sounding at all. "I am very pleased to meet you, sir."

Menefee turned on Weston. "Is this ventriloquist's act somebody's idea of a joke?"

"No joke. Rod told me this morning that he was looking forward to seeing you."

"Actually," the robot continued blandly, "I as yet have some difficulty understanding the concepts humans refer to as 'humor' or 'jokes.'"

"Hmmph!" Menefee stared at Rod as though he didn't quite believe in him.

"And you, sir," Rod said, "are Senator Franklin E. Buchanan."

The robot continued to address each of the visitors in turn, drawing on RAMROD's electronic files for the necessary information. Costrini, meanwhile, had pulled the plug from the receptacle in the robot's side and was sealing up the opening. Working deftly, he ran the head of what looked like an electric soldering iron along the perimeter of the flap of synthetic skin. There was a tiny stink of burning plastic, and no trace of a scar when he was through. "Voilà!" he said, switching off the tool. "If only humans were that easy to repair."

"So in combat," Barbara Roberts said, "if . . . if he

got wounded, you'd just seal him up? I thought he was supposed to be bulletproof."

"Actually," Weston said, "he can change bodies the way we change clothes. This here is what we call Civilian Mod. In half an hour, though, we could switch him to Combat Mod. Turns him into a tank with legs, but he can punch a hole through a concrete-block wall or shake off bullets like a duck shakes off water."

"What?" Menefee said. "You just yank his brain from one body and put it in another?"

"Almost. Actually it's his whole central torso core and his head." Weston tapped Rod's head with a forefinger. The machine did not move or respond to the motion. "Rod's brains aren't up here, you know. They're down here in his chest cavity, heavily shielded and armored. But the head has most of his visual and auditory gear, his balance sensors, and his speech synthesizers. It's easier to leave all that attached when we swap bodies."

"Eh," General Sinclair said, looking nervously at Rod. "You sure we should talk about . . . about *him* that way while he's listening?"

"I don't mind, General Sinclair," Rod said. "I assure you I feel no pain during the process, and I am incapable of suffering from either physiological or psychological shock."

Cautiously, Ashby brought her face close to Rod's once more. "You know, I finally figured out what's been bothering me about him. He doesn't blink!"

Costrini laughed. "I'm afraid there's a glitch there. He's *supposed* to, but there's a fault in the microprocessor chain that handles that subfunction."

"It's not the processors," Dr. McDaniels replied defensively. "It's a problem with the solenoids that trigger the blink reflex."

"Says you. You always blame the mechanical parts."

"Like you always blame the computers."

"Actually," Rod said. "I suspect the malfunction is due to human error."

Weston's eyes widened. He could have sworn that as Rod had spoken, the ghost of a smile had tugged at those otherwise impassive features. Had Rod just tried to make a joke?

He grinned at his own reaction. He'd been at RAMROD for six years now, and *still* the damned thing found ways to surprise him. "Gentlemen, ladies," he said. "Why don't we have a look at Rod in action?" He looked at McDaniels. "Is he ready on that last feed, Doctor?"

"PARET assimilation complete on run three-five-nine," Rod said. From his tone of voice, he might have been discussing the weather. "Systems diagnostic checks complete and satisfactory."

"That means he's ready," McDaniels said. The visitors laughed.

"Tell you what, Roger," Weston said. "Why don't we let Rod give us a little demonstration?"

Luis pulled the telephone van up to the curb in a residential neighborhood, parking just across the street from a modest suburban ranch house. It seemed worlds away from the barrio they'd left half an hour earlier.

"Okay," Luis said. "You know where to go?"

"I got it," the blond-haired man said. "It'll take me a couple hours or so. It's in friggin' Richmond."

"No problem. We'll be here waiting for you."

His companion looked at his watch. "So where the hell are your friends?"

"They'll be along."

"Damn, Luis. How can you be so cool?"

"Perhaps, my friend, I am aware of what will happen if we *lose* our cool." He flicked the stub of his cigarette from the window. "Be calm. It will go well. Diamond knows what he is doing."

The Texan studied the house, then shook his head. "Shit. I hate doing this."

"You don't hate the money, do you? Life's a bitch, man."

"Yeah. And then you die." The Texan opened the door and climbed out of the van. His car, left there earlier, was parked a short distance up the street.

Luis lit another cigarette and continued to watch the front of the house.

☻ Chapter Four

THEY WATCHED THE LARGE MONITOR on Lab One's wall.
Drake could see that the Kiddie Land display screens
had been rearranged, creating a different maze.

"CORA will handle the timing so that it will correspond to the lieutenant's run," McDaniels said. "If Rod
resolves one confrontation quicker than the lieutenant
did, CORA will throw the next one at him that much
faster." She grinned impishly at Drake. "That will give
you a comparison of a Navy SEAL's reflexes with those
of a robot."

"But the maze is different," Tricia Ashby said.
"What will that prove?"

"It proves Rod can respond in a thinking, creative
way," Weston said. "He's not just doing the simulation
by rote. But he'll have the same number of encounters,
the same *kinds* of encounters . . . and the same kinds
of decisions as Lieutenant Drake. Watch now. . . ."

On the monitor, Rod had just entered the maze, clad
now, as Drake had been earlier, in black fatigues and
turtleneck, a .45 automatic in his right hand. He moved
with a fluid, almost catlike grace, though the way his

head turned seemed unnaturally stiff, as though it were scanning.

Costrini switched on a second TV monitor on the wall. "We can tap into Rod's visuals and display them here," he said. "What Rod is seeing, you can see right here." The scene showed the maze from within, overlapping, ceiling-high panels showing streets and buildings. The view shifted left to right, then back again as the robot moved its head. In the upper-right corner were the words STAND BY and TEST SEQUENCE INITIATE: READY.

Ashby's eyebrows arched. "I can't say I'm excited about the prospect of teaching a machine to engage in gunplay like . . . like we saw earlier," she said. "You're expecting a robot to exercise *judgment*?"

"Judgment," Weston said evenly, "is what artificial intelligence is all about. Are we all ready?"

There was a chorus of assents, and one of the techs murmured something into his headset microphone. On the Kiddie Land projection screens, images came to life: a man with a newspaper walking his dog, a woman carrying a baby hidden in a blanket, a postman, two kids playing with cap pistols. Depending on how CORA ran the sim, any of those characters could be armed and dangerous, requiring split-second reflexes and— hell, there was no other word for it—*intuition*.

In combat, Drake always relied on a kind of sixth sense instilled by years of training and several real-life firefights. He'd come to trust that sense. After nearly three months of working with the project, he still didn't see how the hell they could expect to program something like that into a *robot*.

"Time 1528 hours, ten seconds," CORA said from the air overhead. "Simulation three-six-zero. Commence run."

And then Rod's hands blurred as he dragged the slide back on his .45, chambering a round. He moved forward, scanning the screens around him.

Drake glanced at the smaller monitor. The Rod's-eye view showed a targeting reticle superimposed over the moving street scene, the words COMBAT MODE: STAND BY prominent at the upper right. The scene shifted left, centering on a heavyset man in a raincoat. The man turned to face the camera. . . .

The images on the screen exploded into a blur of fire and movement. The man in the raincoat froze motionless, one hand beneath his coat, a hit marker like a bright third eye staring from the bridge of his nose.

But the view was already changing, the motion too quick to follow. Rod was moving with literally inhuman speed and precision, the .45 in his hand barking time and time again in such rapid succession that the shots sounded like they were being fired full auto. There was the briefest of pauses as the empty magazine fell away and a fresh one was rammed home, and then Rod was firing again, twisting and dodging as he acquired targets, tracked, and fired.

"RAMROD Mark I," CORA said. "Run number three-six-zero complete. Time forty-three seconds. Score one hundred percent. No collateral damage."

"I never would've fucking believed it," Menefee said.

Ashby's face was white. "It moved . . . it moved faster than anything I've ever seen."

Menefee looked at Drake. "What do *you* think of all this, Lieutenant? It's your brains they're pickin' for this thing."

"Mine, and those of a few others, sir," Drake said. "Doesn't hurt." He grinned. "Except when I trip over the damned cable to the helmet."

"The point is, you're a SEAL. A professional warrior. What's your opinion of using robots in combat?"

Drake hesitated before answering. His eyes locked with Weston's. "Well, sir," he said slowly, holding Weston's gaze. "I'd have to say that grunts aren't paid to have opinions."

"Look, Roger," Weston said. "It's not a matter of opinion anymore. RAMROD *works* . . . a combat robot that can move, fight, and think faster than a human. It can provide fire support to a human combat team, or go in by itself on missions humans can't handle. When Group Seven became interested in RAMROD, they had the idea that the project might have considerable potential in targeting the drug traffic coming into the U.S. My evaluation is that Rod is ready. He may be exactly the weapon we need to *win* this war, once and for all!"

The DEA man shook his head. "I have two men missing on an OUTCONUS op, James. Emilio Esposito and Ray Calveras. Calveras had a wife and three kids. General Sinclair here lost four of his crack SEALS on the same op. I find it in rather . . . bad taste that you're suggesting we should have sent a machine to the Salazar fortress to do the job, instead of them."

"If we had, maybe they'd still be alive." Weston looked at his watch. "Ladies, gentlemen. I suggest we retire to the third-floor conference room. Perhaps I can answer any other questions you may have there."

Drake stayed in the lab as Weston and the VIPs began moving toward the doors.

Moments after Weston and the others had left, Rod returned to Lab One with Greg Irvin. Drake watched as McDaniels rolled up Rod's sweatshirt so that she and Irvin could get at the robot's access slot.

McDaniels glanced up at Drake as Irvin inserted a power feed. "Okay, Chris," she said archly. "What *do* you think?"

"About what?"

"What they were asking you. Is Rod ready for combat?"

Drake frowned. He'd been mulling over that question since long before Menefee had asked it. Drake had a number of doubts about the whole project, had had them ever since his first day at RAMROD. His personal loyalty to Weston, however, would not have let him admit them to Menefee.

With Heather, though, it was different. They'd worked closely together for most of the past three months, and he knew he could be honest with her. "I wish I could give you a straight answer, Doctor," he said at last. "Oh, he works fine . . . but for combat? Look, when you're in combat, there's a kind of sixth sense, a telepathic instinct that tells you . . ." He let the thought trail off, not sure of what he wanted to say.

"Tells you what?" McDaniels demanded. "We're dealing with science here, Chris, not magic."

"Perhaps Lieutenant Drake is alluding to a certain enhancement of the normal senses," Rod said quietly.

His intrusion into the conversation was so unexpected that Drake almost jumped. Normally, the robot was so still and quiet it was possible to think of it as a totally inanimate machine.

"How do you mean, Rod?" Irvin asked.

"I've scanned a number of references on file here in the RAMROD library and elsewhere," the robot said. "I find frequent mentions of the kind of sixth sense Lieutenant Drake is speaking of. It occurs to me that many of the cases on file could be explained by the normal human senses, particularly those of sight, hearing, and smell. For example, one man might be hiding in a darkened room, watching a second man enter. The second man is not aware of the first, yet might *sense* that something is wrong or that he is being watched."

"He knows he's not alone," McDaniels said.

"Precisely, Dr. McDaniels. Yet that feeling could be attributed to several nonparanormal phenomena. The second man might sense the other's body odor, yet do so on a subliminal level. Perhaps he hears the other man's breathing or detects a change in air pressure as he moves. The clues are enough to raise a suspicion that he is not alone, yet are not strong enough to make themselves clearly recognized for what they are."

"Bull . . . shit," Drake said, enunciating each syllable clearly and precisely.

"You've got a better idea?" McDaniels said, arching one perfect eyebrow.

"I *know* better. Our robot friend here has been reading too many back issues of *Psychology Today*. C'mon, Doc! I've *been* there!"

"You could easily be misinterpreting a perfectly explainable phenomena."

"God, you sound as bad as he does."

"Lieutenant Drake," the robot said. "I am curious about these experiences you mention. Would it be possible to allow me to witness them through the PARET link?"

"Huh?" Drake was taken aback. "Uh . . . you mean PARET my *memories*? That sounds like mind reading."

"In a way he can do just that," McDaniels said. "Same principle as teaching him to use a gun. You remember something, bring it to mind, and he can read the neural firings associated with that memory. In a sense, he's sharing that memory."

"Good God!" Drake said. "And you accuse *me* of talking about magic!"

"Not magic at all," she replied primly. "Rod would have to be familiar with how your brain works . . . which he ought to be by now, after working with you for three months. You'd have to concentrate hard. The process is crude, and he can only deal with clear, clean images. Let your mind wander and he won't be able to read anything."

Drake considered the robot for a moment. The idea appealed to him. "What's your security clearance, Ace?"

"Actually," Rod said, "according to your personnel file, Lieutenant Drake, you are not cleared for that information."

Drake blinked. The damned robot had a higher security clearance than he did! "Right. Aren't you afraid I'll read *your* mind?"

"You can't," McDaniels said. "*Humans* can't. We don't . . ." She stopped and smiled. "We don't have the programming for it."

Drake decided not to press the point. Striding across the lab floor, he picked up a PARET helmet and settled it over his head. "CORA?" he called into the room. "You listening?"

"Monitoring," the RAMROD computer's voice replied from a wall speaker. "PARET direct access initiated . . ."

It had been almost a year, but there was no problem. The memories were as clear, as sharp as if he'd lived them yesterday. . . .

He'd come ashore out of the warm waters of the Gulf, Drake and four other SEALs. Their navigation had been precise. The hulking shape of the Sief Palace rose to their right. To the left, the three spectacular Kuwait City Towers speared the sky.

It was an inky, moonless night and the city was blacked out, but the light-intensifier goggles Drake wore let him see his surroundings with perfect clarity in shades of white and green. Besides, there were fires. Something large was burning beyond the Sief Palace in the direction of the British embassy.

Drake lay in the mud flat on his belly, the water going lap-lap-lap around him. He'd been moving ashore when the Iraqi soldiers—more of a mob than a military formation—had appeared, dragging with them two Kuwaiti girls. He'd given the signal to the others to freeze, then lay there, not moving, scarcely daring to breathe as the Iraqis hunkered down in a circle twenty meters away and started working on their captives.

What followed was the vilest sort of nightmare. The SEALs were under explicit orders. The Iraqis had captured several batteries of deadly HAWK antiaircraft missiles when they invaded Kuwait. Satellite photos had located one battery near the Sief Palace. In waterproof pouches, the SEALs carried circuit boards for the HAWK guidance systems, identical to the boards already in place. . . .

Except that these would melt when the missiles launched.

Once the circuit boards had been replaced, the SEALs would return to the sea for an underwater rendezvous with the SDV that had brought them in. Capture—even discovery and escape—was out of the question, for the enemy could not know they had even been ashore. The SEALs were armed with Mark 22s and their diving knives, far too little firepower to give them a chance against the mob. There was absolutely nothing they could do but wait . . . and watch as the Iraqis raped the Kuwaiti women.

Ten minutes passed . . . then twenty. Another group of soldiers wandered in out of the night, laughing and joking with one another. One of the girls screamed, was silenced by a blow. To move was to risk discovery. If one of the Iraqis even glanced in their direction . . .

A soldier stood with a grunt, a comic-horror figure wearing only his shirt, an AK-47 slung muzzle down across his back. He gave his victim a mocking salute and a gap-toothed leer, then turned and started walking down the beach, coming toward the SEALs.

Drake tensed, Hush Puppy ready in his hand. If he had to fire, the five of them would have to bolt for the water. There'd be no continuing the mission once the alarm was raised.

The Iraqi soldier came closer, four meters away. Drake heard the squelch of his bare feet in the mud. Raising his head, he found himself looking squarely into the Iraqi's eyes.

The fire on the skyline seemed impossibly bright, and the foul air carried the tang of burning oil. For an endless moment, SEAL and Iraqi looked at each other, across a distance of a few feet.

Had he been seen? Drake couldn't tell. The Iraqi seemed to be looking straight at him, eyes narrowing as if trying to make out some dimly seen shape in the darkness. A motion, a breath would betray the SEAL. The Iraqi would die . . . but not before he screamed warning to two dozen friends at his back.

Drake's finger tightened on the pistol's trigger . . . then eased. His eyes, already narrowed to slits to hide the whites, dropped away from the other man's. They taught you in the Sneaky Pete courses that staring at another man could warn him that you were there, that he could feel you watching him. Rock, Drake thought. I'm a rock . . . a rock . . . a rock. . . . He focused his eyes on the man's hands. There was blood on them, and a gold ring too large for his finger.

The Iraqi snorted, brushed aside his shirttail, and began urinating into the Gulf.

The release of tension was almost too much to bear. Drake was certain the Iraqi had seen something . . . and had then decided it was nothing.

One of the women was screaming again, weakly this time, pleading. The Iraqi finished what he was doing, then turned away from the water and stalked back up the beach.

Eventually, the soldiers gathered their weapons and

*clothing and wandered off. The SEALs moved away from
the water, carried out their mission, and returned an hour
later to the mud flat. Before they donned rebreathers and
masks, Drake looked for the women to see if there was anything he could do.*

Both were already dead.

Drake removed the helmet, blinking at the brilliance
of the overhead lights in the lab and breathing deeply.
For a moment, it was almost as though he'd been reliv-
ing the incident. "Well," he said, and his voice
cracked. He cleared his throat. "Well, Rod?"

"Fascinating," the robot said. "And is it your con-
tention that the soldier did not see you because you tele-
pathically convinced him you were a rock?"

Drake laughed. "No. But for a moment, it did feel
as though I could . . . *read* him. Feel him, feel his
thoughts. One moment I was ready to kill him. The next
moment, I knew he hadn't seen me, that it was okay.
And . . . I'm convinced the bit about not looking at the
guy works. I was staring right at him, and he was definitely uneasy. I looked down, and he relaxed."

"Sounds pretty subjective to me, Lieutenant,"
McDaniels said.

"You weren't there, Doctor. What do you think,
Rod?"

"I do not know, Lieutenant Drake. But you have
given me a great deal to think about. Thank you."

Quitting time at RAMROD was 1700 hours. Two
hours after the session with Rod, Chris Drake changed
into his civilian clothes in the building's first-floor
locker room, then picked up his car, a red Alliance, in
the basement garage and checked out through Camp

Peary's main gate. Following the signs for Yorktown
and Hampton, he merged into the traffic flow on Inter-
state 64 South where it passed the base perimeter two
miles from Williamsburg.

As always at this time of day, the traffic was murder-
ous.

Christopher Drake had joined the Navy in the late
seventies, after two years of trying to support a wife
and newborn baby while going to college by day and
working in a warehouse at night. After boot camp, and
for no better reason than determination to prove himself, he'd volunteered for BUD/S training and been accepted. He spent fifteen weeks of hellish training at
Coronado, somehow avoiding the course's eighty-
percent dropout rate, and won the coveted trident pin
of a Navy SEAL in 1979. When SEAL Team Six was
organized as the Navy's antiterrorist unit in 1980,
Drake volunteered for special training with Delta Force
at Fort Bragg.

In 1985, Palestinian terrorists hijacked the liner
Achille Lauro and, along the way, murdered an eighty-
year-old American tourist in his wheelchair. Drake had
been one of the Navy SEALs readying for an assault
against the terrorists. Later, he'd been present when
Navy F-14s forced the aircraft of terrorist mastermind
Abu Abbas to land at Sigonella. Watching the Italian
authorities set free the man who had planned the *Achille Lauro* hijacking had filled Drake with a towering
rage.

He almost quit.

His response was typical of a man who refused to
be beaten by the system. Instead of resigning, he ap-

plied for an officer candidate program and became a mustang, an officer who'd come up through the ranks.

As a SEAL lieutenant j.g., then, he'd participated in the reorganization of the SEALs, transferring to SEAL Team Eight when that unit, its very existence classified, had taken on most of the Navy's antiterrorist responsibilities. In 1989 he participated in the takedown of terrorists occupying an oil rig in the Gulf of Mexico, an operation that went so smoothly the incident never even made the newspapers. A year later, a newly promoted lieutenant, he'd found himself in another Gulf, on a mission so sensitive he wasn't even supposed to tell his wife.

And after that had come his assignment to RAM-ROD. Three months now of light duty and no watches . . . except for the quick sneak-and-peak into Colombia with SNOWDROP a week ago.

SEAL Eight's permanent station was Dam Neck, Virginia, tucked away on the southern shore of Chesapeake Bay between Norfolk and Virginia Beach, a part of the Little Creek Amphibious Base. Rather than subjecting his wife and daughter to what was euphemistically referred to as "substandard base housing" with a two-year waiting list, Drake had rented a ranch-style house in Virginia Beach. Normally, on nights when he didn't have the duty, he had a fifteen-minute drive home. Since he'd been TAD'd to RAMROD, though, his evening commute ran closer to an hour and a half, and even that depended on how badly the traffic was backed up at the Hampton Roads Bridge-Tunnel. It was forty miles from Williamsburg to Virginia Beach, following the expressway through Newport News, Hampton, then across the Roads to Norfolk.

Norfolk was the largest U.S. Navy base in the world. One hundred twenty thousand military personnel worked there, or in the nearby facilities at Portsmouth, Little Creek, Dam Neck, or the naval air station at Oceana, all supported by over forty thousand civilian employees. And at rush hour, every one of them hit the highways. He gripped the steering wheel of the Alliance in growing frustration as the line of traffic crawled into the tunnel portion of the Hampton Roads Bridge-Tunnel.

He was especially eager to get home to Meagan and their daughter Stacy tonight. His sudden arrival back from Panama the day before had ended their agony of several days, knowing that he was missing, not knowing if he was dead. Sinclair himself had visited them as soon as word was radioed from *Decisive* that he'd been recovered, but the real relief, for all of them, had come yesterday afternoon when he met them at Oceana.

Meagan had pulled Stacy out of school for the occasion. At thirteen, Stacy was old enough to know what MIA meant. The two of them had been waiting on the runway when the C-130 Hercules taxied to a stop.

They'd planned a homecoming celebration—dinner out at a favorite restaurant—but first had come his debriefing at the hands of several CIA spook types. He'd come home late that night, exhausted, his time in the jungle finally catching up with him, and knowing that he had to get up early the next day for more debriefings with Sinclair and Weston.

So they'd decided that their celebration would be tonight, Friday night.

The traffic was moving faster now as he emerged from the depths of the Roads Tunnel and onto the broad ribbon of highway spanning the southern half of Hampton Roads. Below him, the late afternoon sun danced and sparkled on the water. Twenty more minutes and he'd be home.

Meagan. His thoughts turned again to his wife. He'd been so tired last night he scarcely remembered their time in bed, but it seemed that he could still feel her caresses as she'd drawn him close.

Lovely, raven-haired Meagan Drake had put up with a hell of a lot as a Navy wife. As they both were fond of saying, it was a damn good thing she loved him. A bumper sticker seen frequently on automobiles in the Norfolk area told it all: "Navy Wife—It's the toughest job in the Navy!"

The separations were the worst, especially the unexpected ones that began with a phone call in the night. More often than not, he hadn't even been able to tell Meagan where he was going, and only rarely could he say when he'd be coming home.

Somehow, though, she always seemed to know. Combat vets weren't the only ones to know and use that sixth-sense instinct.

Off the bridge now, he took the Northampton Boulevard exit, escaping the slow-moving base traffic on 64 and swinging into the suburban arrays of neat homes and small yards along Cape Henry Street not far from the spires of Virginia Wesleyan College. He turned the Alliance into his driveway, set the brake, and got out.

A C&P van was parked across the street. He wondered if the neighbors were having phone problems. Nearby were several motorcycles he didn't remember seeing before.

Curious. This was a quiet neighborhood, usually—quiet if you discounted the fact that it lay under the traffic approach lanes to Norfolk International. Pocketing his car keys, he strode up the flagstone walkway, opened the front door, and stepped inside.

"Hey, Meg!" he called, walking into the living room. "Where's my lover?"

Then something smashed against the base of his neck, catapulting him forward onto the carpet, red-shot blackness exploding inside his skull.

Somewhere, very far away, someone was screaming.

⟨ᴍ⟩ *Chapter Five*

DRAKE BLINKED THROUGH WAVES of pain, trying to clear his head, trying to *see*. He knew he'd been unconscious, but he had no way of knowing how long. He was lying facedown on the living room carpet, the nap of the rug pressed uncomfortably against his cheek and nose. He tried to move and felt the cold pinch of steel against his wrists. His hands were handcuffed behind his back, and his ankles were pinned by something tough, rope or tape of some sort.

"Well, well," a voice said from above and behind him. "Our SEAL friend is alive after all!"

The voice was familiar . . . and a growing, surprised horror gnawed its way up from the pit of Drake's stomach. Ignoring the pain in his head, he rolled to the side until he could prop himself up on one elbow, and found himself looking up into a well-known face.

"Esposito!" The last time he'd seen the DEA man had been in the jungle clearing, seconds before the helicopter opened fire on the SNOWDROP SEAL team. "You're . . . dead!"

He realized as soon as the words were out how silly that sounded. If Esposito was alive, here, it could only mean that he had been in on the Colombian ambush. Drake had not, after all, actually *seen* the man killed.

"As they say, my friend, the reports of my death have been greatly exaggerated," Esposito said, rubbing his mustache. "Unfortunately, I'm afraid that yours will not be."

"Chris!"

Meagan's voice!

He wrenched himself around, horror mounting. There were four other men there, seedy, gutter-slime types in biker jackets and gang colors. Two, at least, had MAC-10 subguns. They were standing in the archway that connected the dining room with the living room. One held Meagan from behind, one arm pressed across her chest. Another held Stacy. Both mother and daughter had their hands tied behind them and were struggling against their captors.

"Meagan!" he gasped. "Stacy!" He twisted around to face Esposito. "You bastard! Let them go! Whatever your problem is, it's with me, not them!"

Esposito continued smiling, his handsome Latin face maddeningly out of reach. "It's a shame to have to involve your wife and daughter, I know. I'm truly sorry it has to be this way. But we have to make your death look accidental, you know." He chuckled. " 'Accidental' may be the wrong word. Let's say . . . 'misleading.' "

The thug holding Stacy reached around and began kneading her breasts through her T-shirt. She screamed and tried to pull away. "Hey, boss," he said, laughing. "When does the fun start?"

"Patience, Julio. We're waiting for a friend of mine.

You'll get your fun after we've tended to business. Why don't you put them down over there, then give the rest of us a hand?"

Roughly, the invaders shoved Meagan and Stacy onto the living room couch. One of them stood guard with a MAC-10 Ingram while the others vanished into other parts of the house. Drake could hear them moving about, and once he heard the metallic clang of a metal grate.

To Drake, it sounded like the grillwork over the forced-air heating ducts in the hall. Were they looking for something? What?

The sounds grew more violent, and once there was a crash that sounded like a ceiling lighting fixture being broken, followed by the dry, crumbling noise of broken plaster.

"God, Chris!" Meagan said. Her face betrayed her terror. "Oh God, Chris! Who are these people? You . . . you know one of them?"

"Yeah, I know him."

He hitched himself up to a sitting position, his eyes on the thug they'd left standing guard in the living room. The guy was in his early twenties, Drake guessed, wearing blue jeans and a tank top, with his long black hair pulled back in a ponytail. He was ponderously overweight, his beer belly hanging over the belt of his jeans. Brand-new cowboy boots graced his feet, and he held his MAC-10 with studied nonchalance.

"But who *is* he?" Meagan asked. "Where did you—"

"Look, honey," Drake said. He was terribly aware

of what Esposito had said about a *misleading* death. "If
you don't know, maybe I can convince them to let you
go. So no questions, okay? Just stay calm. It'll be all
right."

But he knew it was not going to be all right. Why
had Esposito shown himself? Drake had thought the
man was dead, and if the DEA man had stayed out of
sight, the SEAL would have kept on believing that.

So there was more to it than that, something important enough to make Esposito try to murder not only
Drake, but Meagan and Stacy as well.

There was another loud crash from one of the bedrooms, then another. It sounded like they were using
something heavy as a sledgehammer, to open up the
wall.

"Daddy!" Stacy called from the couch. He could tell
from her voice that she was on the ragged edge of panic.
"Daddy, they're in my room! What do they *want*?"

"I don't know, sweetheart," he said. He kept his
eyes on the guard.

The man took no notice of the destructive sounds
coming from elsewhere in the house, but he leered at
Stacy when she spoke, then walked over until he was
standing over her. "I want you, little *puta*!" he said.
He grabbed his crotch with his free hand and pumped
his hips back and forth, brutally suggestive. "I'm going
to have you, too!"

"Cool it, King Kong!" Drake barked. "Your argument is with me!"

The fat thug only laughed and reached for Stacy's
leg. She was wearing cutoff shorts, and his hand

grabbed her bare thigh, eliciting a scream of pure horror.

"Get your hands off her!" Meagan yelled. *"You bastard! Leave her alone!"*

The guard whipped his hand around and struck Meagan across the mouth. "Silence, woman! I've got something for you, too, don't worry!"

Driven by pure, burning rage, Drake lunged forward. With his hands and feet bound, he only managed an uncontrolled crash into the man's leg, making their tormentor stagger back a step. Drake caught a blurred impression of one of the man's cowboy boots snapping up toward his head. The blow caught him in the side of the face, stunning him, leaving him lying on his back with a roaring sound in his ears, his vision blurred, the pain in his head hammering away like naval gunfire.

"Enough, Ramón. Enough!" Esposito's voice said. "Now, now, Lieutenant Drake. You should have saved your heroics for the jungle."

Drake blinked his eyes open and looked up into Esposito's cold eyes. "Listen," he said. His voice, his breath rasped in his throat. He licked his lips, trying to bring moisture to them. "Listen, please," he said again. He was desperate now, desperate for the lives of his girls. He knew in that moment that he would do anything, *anything* to save them. *Anything* . . .

"The girls don't know you," he said. "They don't know anything about you. They can't hurt you! Let them go . . . *please*. . . ."

Esposito sighed and slowly shook his head. "You know, if only you'd had the grace to die in Colombia, none of this would have been necessary." He spread his hands, as though helpless. "As it is, we do what we have to do."

The three other intruders were back, methodically wrecking the house. They turned each large piece of upholstered furniture over, slashing with knives, pulling out the stuffing. They didn't seem to be looking for anything. The destruction itself appeared to be all that mattered.

Esposito vanished for a moment into another room, then returned carrying a brick-size plastic bag filled with white powder and wrapped in tape. He was wearing leather gloves, concerned, apparently, about leaving fingerprints. Fumbling with the package a moment, he broke it open. White powder as fine as baking soda spilled on the carpet, misted the air. Cocaine, Drake thought. It can't be anything else. . . .

"Hey, man!" one of the thugs, a lanky kid with one earring and a Grateful Dead T-shirt, protested. "That's prime jam, man! Why you throwin' it away?"

"Here." Esposito tossed the half-empty bag at the kid. "Knock yourself out."

"Outta sight, man." The kid unslung his MAC, then dumped the remaining powder on the glass top of the dining room table.

Drake heard the sound of a car pulling up outside. Moments later, the front door banged open, and another man walked into the living room carrying a gym bag. Drake did not recognize him, a stocky man with blond hair. Like Esposito he was wearing gloves. "Got it," the newcomer said.

"Any problems?"

"No sweat, Luis." He opened the gym bag and extracted another MAC-10, handing it to Esposito. "It was hidden away in that little old storehouse, just like you said."

Drake's mind was racing, horror and revelation pursuing one another in tightening circles of madness. The newcomer spoke with an easy drawl, a Texan accent. . . .

Like the voice he'd heard on the radio while waiting for a dust-off in a Colombian field.

And he'd called Esposito Luis.

But the name was Emilio. Emilio Esposito of the DEA.

Esposito checked the weapon. "Okay, Chaco," he said, addressing an evil-looking thug with a heavy beard. "Time to go. You have it all straight?"

"Sure, boss." He grinned through the beard. "Thirty minutes, then let 'em all have it."

"Bueno." He handed Chaco the MAC-10. "Be certain you use *this* weapon. Kill them all at the same time, drop the gun, and run before the neighbors can call the police."

Chaco squinted at Esposito suspiciously. "You sure the cops won't trace this to us, man?"

"Hey, Chaco!" Esposito said. "You're my main man! We wouldn't let any shit happen to you!"

"How come the special chatterbox, then?"

"That subgun," Esposito said, "was used to pop a crack dealer in Richmond last week. When the cops find it here, they'll figure the same guys did it."

"What about fingerprints, man?" He didn't sound convinced.

"So wipe it off when you're done! We just want the

ballistics to match, man, okay? Cops'll call it a gangland drug killing and let it go." He reached out and
patted Chaco's face. "Don't sweat it!"

"Piece a cake," the fat guy, Ramón, said. "The Feds
won't have a thing on us, hombre. We'll be long gone!"

"Yeah . . ."

"So finish up here. When you're done, meet us at
the usual place and you'll get the rest of the money."
Esposito clapped Chaco's shoulder, then handed him
another packet of white powder, a smaller one this
time, containing at best a few ounces. "Meanwhile,
enjoy yourselves. Have a blast."

Chaco grinned, pocketing the coke. "Okay, man.
Pleasure doin' business with you."

Esposito paused, then walked over to where Drake
was lying on the floor, still recovering from the kick
in the head. He squatted and patted Drake's shoulder.
"Listen, guy. Nothing personal, okay?"

"You son-of-a-bitch bastard!" Drake lunged, trying
to strike him, to *hurt* him. . . .

"Hey!" the blond man called from the doorway.
"C'mon, Luis! Let's haul ass, for Chrissakes! Diamond
doesn't want us anywhere around when this goes down,
okay?"

"Go on, then!" Esposito stood again. "Anyway, Lieutenant, sorry it had to be like this. Just business, you
know?" He turned and walked away. Drake heard the
front door slam, followed a few moments later by the
sound of engines starting up outside.

"Time for some fun now, eh, Chaco?"

"Keep your fly zipped, Ramón. We gotta slice up the

couch. You and Julio take the bitches into the bedroom. Arturo and me . . . hey, Arturo!''

The skinny guy looked up from the dining room table. He'd already emptied the powder onto the glass and was using his knife to create lines of the stuff.

''Get the fuck over here, Arturo,'' Chaco ordered. ''Do that shit later. Help me with the sofa.''

Julio and Ramón dragged Meagan and Stacy out of the room as Drake struggled into an upright position against the wall. Arturo and Chaco ignored him, concentrating on overturning the sofa. Using pocketknives, they began slitting the bottom, revealing the springs.

Breathing hard now with fear and exertion, Drake took stock of the situation. His hands were secured in handcuffs. That wouldn't be a large problem; he was in excellent physical shape, lean and agile. The chain on the cuffs was long enough that he would have no problem working his hips through the circle of his arms, then drawing his knees and feet through. That would get his hands in front of his body where he could use them.

His feet were another matter. They'd strapped them together with a heavy gray tape . . . duct tape, he thought. He'd need a knife to cut it.

Chaco straightened, folding his jackknife and stuffing it in his pocket. ''Watch our friend here, Arturo,'' he said. ''I'd better see if Ramón and Julio need any help with the *putas*!'' He winked cheerfully at Drake, rubbing his crotch, then walked out of the room whistling, his MAC-10 casually slung over his shoulder.

Arturo stood there, watching Drake incuriously for minute after agonizing minute. The SEAL could hear the sounds from one of the bedrooms, just a short way down the hallway out of the dining room, and wished to God that he could not. Stacy crying, Meagan pleading. One of their captors laughed, a harsh bark filled with malice.

"Look, Arturo," Drake said. "You know you can't get away with this. Help me, and I'll make it worth your while!"

"Oh shit," Arturo said, smirking. "Gimme a break, man!" He watched his prisoner for several more minutes as the sounds from the bedroom grew more strident, more desperate.

"Hey, Chaco!" a voice called. *"This one's prime, hey?"*

Suddenly Arturo seemed to lose interest. He sniffed loudly, then walked back to the dining room table, sitting down with his back to the helpless SEAL. He seemed more interested in the cocaine than in guard duty, and for that, Drake was very, very grateful.

His eyes on Arturo's back, Drake began squeezing his shackled wrists down past his buttocks. His head still throbbing from the earlier abuse, he fought back tears and dizziness as he tried not to make any noise.

"Leave her alone!" Meagan screamed in the bedroom. *"For God's sake, she's just a baby!"*

"Silencio, puta!" There was another scream, wordless this time.

Drake's wrists slid behind his knees. Arturo had his face down close to the table. He inhaled, snorted, then leaned back, wiping his nose with a finger. An Ingram was lying on the table beside his elbow. Drake could see it, could see a trickle of sweat on the back of Arturo's neck. *Oh, help me, God! Help me help me help me . . . !*

He would kill them . . . kill them all with his bare hands if he had to. He tried the tape on his ankles. It was tough, like plastic packing tape. He would never free it with his hands.

Arturo was seated perhaps fifteen feet away, his back still turned to Drake. Silently, using every ounce of skill in stealthy movement available to the SEAL, Drake pulled himself toward the lanky gang member. The screams from the bedroom were subsiding now, but they still were loud enough to cover the rasp of his trousers dragging across the carpet.

"Hey, hurry it up, compadre! I can't wait much longer, man!"

Three feet away now, Drake steadied himself on his hands, drawing his legs beneath him, rising unsteadily to his feet. His eyes still on Arturo's back, he saw the man's shoulder muscles bunch, as though he was suddenly aware of movement behind him.

Drake's hands snapped out together, grabbing Arturo's hair in viselike grips on either side of his head, just above his ears. Using all his strength, he slammed the cokehead's face forward, onto the glass tabletop.

There was a loud pop as glass cracked. Drake hauled Arturo's head back, the face a mask of blood, then slammed it forward again . . . and again. Blood dissolved smeared lines of white powder in the spiderweb cracks in the glass. Gently, Drake lowered the body to the floor.

Quickly now. He took Arturo's knife and freed his ankles, then grabbed the MAC-10. He checked the magazine, a bit clumsily with his hands still cuffed. The mag felt full, and one round was already chambered. Idiot . . . carrying the vicious little auto weapon around with a loaded chamber . . .

Weapon at the ready, Drake sprinted down the hall. The door to one of the bedrooms—his and Meagan's—was closed, the sounds from behind it much weaker now, interspersed with laughter and a heart-sickening grunting noise that whipped Drake to a trembling fury.

It was not vengeance that drove him so much as survival. Training and experience both had taught him long ago that the choreographed firefights staged on Hollywood's screens had little in common with reality. Taking them one-on-three was an act of pure desperation, but it was either try . . . or he, Meagan, and Stacy were going to die. His one hope was that they'd put down their MAC-10s, that he could catch them unarmed. He'd have a chance then, unless something terribly wrong happened.

It happened five paces from the door. "Whee-oo!" someone called from inside. "Hey, Arturo! Get the fuck in here and have some!" Julio banged through the door, Ingram pointed at the ceiling, hitching up his jeans with his free hand. "These honeys are _sweet!_" There was no time to think, no time for anything fancy. Drake's finger tightened on the MAC-10's trigger, snapping a short, buzzsaw burst into the drugger's sleeveless undershirt.

Drake plowed over the man's body before it had time to fall, bursting into the bedroom and a scene of nightmare horror.

They'd torn this room apart, too, overturning the

dresser, slashing the big queen-size mattress. Stacy and Meagan were tied to the bed side by side, naked, spread-eagled by strips of cloth cut from their clothing. Ramón was between Meagan's legs, obscenely naked, grossly fat, rising to his knees at the sound of gunfire in the hall. Chaco was on the far side of the bed, next to Stacy. He had just snatched an Ingram from the bedside table and was swinging it up to cover the door.

Drake fired again. The man with the gun was the threat, the primary target, but 9mm rounds slammed into Ramón's quivering bulk as Drake dragged the muzzle around, straining to hit Chaco before the gunman was able to fire. Too late! Chaco fired at almost the same instant, the muzzle flash stabbing from his weapon in the mercifully dim-lit bedroom. He'd not had time to aim. Chaco's first shots hammered into the bed as he screamed.

"No!" Drake's own scream of denial and rage and terror mingled with Chaco's agony. Ramón pitched backward off the bed, blood from three wounds splattering ceiling, walls, and floor as he fell. Chaco was slammed against the wall, leaving bloody tracks where the fingers of one hand clawed at the paint. The MAC-10 in the gunman's other hand kept firing wildly, slamming rounds into the door, the wall, the bed. . . .

He collapsed facedown across Stacy, the Ingram spilling from his grasp.

For one horrible moment, Drake stood there in a room suddenly gone death silent. There was blood everywhere . . . *everywhere,* painting the walls in slashes of scarlet, pooling on the bed, drooling from Ramón's chest. His Ingram, the magazine empty, dropped to the floor, the clatter unbearably loud in the sudden quiet.

Meagan had turned her head toward him as he entered the room. Her eyes were glassy now, unseeing, the luxuriant spill of black hair across the pillow matted with blood and pieces of skull. The side of her head nearest Drake had been blown away. Next to her, Stacy lay still with eyes closed. When Drake rolled the corpse off her body, he saw the savage wounds cratering her chest in a neat, straight line where Chaco's unaimed fire had walked across her, puncturing heart and lungs like the vicious stabs of an ice pick.

Drake's scream of anguish and pain rang from the bloody walls, echoed down the hallway.

He did not leave their bodies for a long, long time.

● Chapter Six

It was Sunday. The Salazar family had just returned from Mass at *La Catedral* in Santa Marta, but the big, midday meal was still several hours away. The rich aroma of *cazuela de mariscos*—a thick stew of various seafoods—hung heavy in the humid air. The sun was bright and hot, but there was just enough breeze off the sea to make the partially shaded patio attractive.

Above the pool, the verdant rise of the Sierra Nevada de Santa Marta rose in towering splendor to the south, the tallest peaks capped with snow glistening in the noon sun. The northern slopes of those mountains grew some of the finest marijuana in the world, and much of that land belonged to the Salazars.

That marijuana had been the beginnings of the Salazar empire, back before the world had gone crazy for coke.

José Salazar walked onto the pool-side flagstones, a cup of coffee in hand. His uncle Roberto was already on the patio, leaning back in a lounge chair with a glass of *aguardiente*, watching the antics of three naked girls splashing in the pool. The girls were not regular residents of the hacienda, but Roberto occasionally had them flown in from Bogotá, as entertainment for certain guests. A special visitor was arriving, one who had enjoyed Roberto's hospitality on several earlier occasions. The aircraft, an old C-123 Provider air transport, had swept low over the hacienda, circled, and touched down at the airstrip to the east only minutes before. José had just come from the hacienda's radio room, where he'd spoken with the pilot and given orders for the loading of the cargo.

"Qué ha hecho, Tío Roberto," he said, sinking into a chair at his uncle's side.

"Hello, José. Our friend is down?"

"Sí, mi tío. He will be here shortly." José frowned. "I do not trust this *norteamericano."*

"And you think that I do? Still, it is a remarkable thing that we have achieved here, nephew. *Qué putería!"* The expression, a vulgar Colombian expletive, could refer to something either very good or very bad, but in any case, wildly fantastic or improbable. It was clear that Roberto was pleased with himself. He laughed. "Did you see the look on old Don Fabio's face when I told him that American SEALs were coming to the party the other night? I thought he would have a stroke, right there on the spot!"

"I enjoyed watching their faces the next day, Uncle. When we took them out to the jungle to see the bodies." José grinned. "You were showing off, Uncle Roberto. Shamelessly."

"I made my point, no?" He gestured toward the hacienda. "That the Salazars have the advantage in what the army would call military intelligence. I think we will be able to do business with them now."

José watched the girls in silence for a while. He did not agree, but it was never politic to contradict the old man, not directly, at any rate.

It was Roberto's dream, José knew, to unite the mutually hostile Colombian cartels under one family. A self-proclaimed expert on criminal history, Roberto was fond of pointing out that the splintered, battling Chicago gangs of the twenties had gone nowhere until they were united, working together in a true syndicate instead of fighting among themselves. José, who had traveled in America, who had done business with the ruling mafiosi of Chicago and other cities, knew that the truth was more complex, and brutal: it was the gang wars that had united the American syndicates in the first place. The modern-day Mafia empire of Chicago's Tony Accardo was a direct, lineal descendant of the gangland mobs of Alfonso Capone and Frank Nitti.

And more than that, the gang battles continued to this day. It was simply that the killings received little national attention in the press. Not like the bloodletting in Colombia, where *El Espectador* published lists of the victims each week and demanded that the government take action.

How long, he wondered, before the killings in the United States grew to match the proportions of the slaughter in his own country? It was not that José enjoyed the killings. For him, the murders, the hits, the kidnappings and tortures were simply business.

It was a matter of economics. Coca leaves sold in Colombia for perhaps fifty cents a kilo, a price that fluctuated with government attempts—never more than marginally successful—to burn or capture the crops.

A thousand kilos of leaves were required for one kilo of eighty-percent-pure cocaine . . . but that kilo sold on the streets of Miami or New York or Chicago for anywhere from twenty to sixty thousand dollars, depending on availability.

That made cocaine, gram for gram, up to four times more valuable than its weight in gold.

It made cocaine worth killing for, as rival families struggled to control the pipelines into the United States. America's demand for the white powder seemed inexhaustible, but there were only so many ways to get it past Customs agents and the Border Patrol, Coast Guard cutters, and AWACS radar planes. It was the pipelines that made the drug lords vulnerable, the pipelines that they fought and died for. It was the pipelines that the enemy, the DEA and other antinarcotics organizations, kept trying to penetrate.

The cocaine trade in Colombia was dominated by several major syndicates, or cartels, of *narcotrafficantes*. The largest, without question, was the Medellín cartel, with the Calí organization a close number two. Like the Sicilian Mafia, the cartels tended to be dominated by particular families—security was less of a problem when you were dealing with sons and nephews and cousins—and as with the Mafia, terror and money were the two principal weapons that kept them secure.

Terror guaranteed that witnesses would not testify, prosecutors would not take cases, jurists would not sit, judges would not convict. The terror had reached the proportions of all-out war and generated a new word: *narcoterrorist*. In Medellín alone, a city with a population of two million, there had been over five thousand drug-related murders in 1990.

But money was in many ways even more powerful than terror. Money *bought* terror—Medellín's chief of police had lost 215 agents in just the first four months after the *narcotrafficantes* put a four-thousand-dollar bounty on each policeman slain—but money bought other things as well. Things such as policemen, who typically earned $140 a month, including hazardous-duty pay. Prosecutors. Judges. Army officers. Members of F-2, the army's undercover investigative unit. High-ranking officers of the DAS. Politicians in Colombia. Politicians in the United States.

José had personally delivered hefty campaign contributions to more than one American congressman on his trips to the U.S. One "contribution" had guaranteed the lifting of restrictions on the export of ether—vital for the processing of cocaine base. Another had blocked the military appropriations that would have upgraded the search radars used by U.S. Coast Guard vessels. The reach of the cartels into the very lifeblood of the United States was growing each week.

And in Colombia, the drug lords had all but won. That was not to say that the government was controlled by the drug lords. Quite the contrary, in fact, for Bogotá had viciously escalated the campaign against the cartels. *Los Extraditables*, as they called themselves—those subject to extradition and prosecution by the United States—had been hurt badly in the last few years by government crackdowns, raids, and arrests. Many of the biggest *narcotrafficantes*, the Ochoas and

Pablo Escobar among them, were on the run now and had lost much of their personal fortunes.

But the idea was not to dominate the entire government, but only to control certain key points. One of these points was Colonel Delgado, a high-ranking officer of the *Departmento Administrativo de Seguridad*, Colombia's equivalent of the American FBI. The DAS was deeply involved in combating the cocaine cartels; more to the point, it worked closely with various agencies in the United States, including both the DEA and the CIA. By buying Delgado, Roberto had established a link with someone in Washington, someone known only by the code name *Diamante*—Diamond.

Who Diamond was, *what* he was, José didn't know, but he did know that Delgado had made the first contact, setting up the network by which Diamond could communicate with the Salazars. A great deal of critical information had already passed from Washington to Colombia, timely intelligence on CIA and DEA operations and surveillance plans.

Diamond, and the recent difficulties experienced by the Medellín and Calí cartels, had given Roberto his great opportunity. The summit last week had been called to make the other cartel families an offer: work together under the Salazars, and the Salazars would provide to all the benefits of their intelligence network in Washington. The ambush of the SEALs had been orchestrated, through Delgado and his links with the DEA, to provide an effective and convincing demonstration.

And today they would initiate the second part of Roberto's plan. Diamond had provided the Salazars with another contact, a gringo with impressive connections within America's Central Intelligence Agency itself. Michael Howard Braden was a pilot—of both fixed- and rotary-winged aircraft—and he had flown hundreds of missions throughout Latin America under contract for the CIA. For a percentage of Diamond's profits, he would open a new cocaine pipeline into the United States, one which the Coast Guard and customs and the DEA would never be able to interdict.

For a *narcotrafficante*, it was a dream come true.

It was a bold idea . . . and a dangerous one. By using codes and security procedures that he, as a CIA contract flier, had access to, Braden had promised to fly unprecedented amounts of cocaine directly into the United States, using, of all things, American military transport aircraft and bases. Today's flight would be a test of that promise. If it worked, the Salazars would have a second inducement to the other cartels—a secure way of flying ton after ton of white gold into the gringos' heartland, with the Americans' unknowing cooperation!

Que putería!

But in José Salazar's opinion, cooperation with the other cartels would be short-lived. Sooner or later the Salazars would have to eliminate their old competitors.

And Diamond would give them the key to do so, making *La Familia Salazar* the unrivaled masters of the Colombian cocaine trade.

José, *El Tiburón*, knew it was only a matter of time.

One of the Salazar Land Rovers pulled up on the driveway, not far from the hedge-bordered patio. Their guest climbed out and approached, carrying a large attaché case and accompanied by two of Roberto's Uzi-armed bodyguards. José stood, watching suspiciously. Roberto remained in the lounge chair.

"Howdy, Don Roberto," the man said in his easy, drawled English as the two bodyguards took up unobtrusive positions nearby. A third watched from the second-story deck extending from the east wing of the house above the pool. Ignoring the display of weapons, the visitor offered his hand. "Hey, José. What's cookin'?"

"Mr. Braden," Roberto said in English, shaking the American's hand. "A pleasure to see you again. I trust you had a enjoyable flight?"

"Smooth, Don Roberto. Smooth as that chick's ass over there." He gestured across the pool toward where one of the girls had climbed out of the water and was sunbathing on a towel. "I see you laid in my favorite entertainment."

"Of course." Roberto laughed. "My wife does not approve, but for a friend such as yourself, nothing is too good." He sighed. "But, business first. What of the . . . problem?"

"Taken care of, Bobby. The SEAL who escaped was debriefed, but Diamond managed to handle the classification of the report. It won't be a problem. And the SEAL, he's dead now. He won't be identifying anybody."

"There were no, ah, loose ends?"

Braden grinned. "Nope. We used local muscle. We were gonna hit them ourselves, but the police beat us to it. There aren't any loose ends left. Not anymore."

"Perfecto," Roberto said, relaxing somewhat. He

nodded toward the suitcase. "And you have something to show me there?"

Braden laid the case on a pool-side table and snapped it open. It was filled with neatly ordered stacks of money, U.S. hundred- and thousand-dollar bills. "Like we agreed, Don Roberto," Baden said as José began counting it. "Half down—five million. Your boys are loading the flake onto my plane now. Tonight, I'll be off. With a refueling stop in Florida, the stuff'll be in Washington by tomorrow morning. Next week, I'll be back here with the rest of the money for that load, plus down payment for the next shipment." He pursed his lips. "A sweet deal, amigo. While the DEA and Coasties are knocking themselves out chasing Beechcraft and Aztecs carrying a few hundred kilos, we'll be funneling the stuff in five, ten tons at a clip."

"A sweet deal for you, Señor Braden, since you are purchasing the product at . . . how do you say? Bargain-basement prices."

"Aw, c'mon, Bobby! We're all gonna get filthy rich with this new deal, and you know it!"

The current price for eighty-percent-pure cocaine smuggled into the United States was twenty thousand dollars a kilo. Braden's organization was paying half that, ten thousand a kilo, knowing that they could cut the product with lactose, turning one kilo into two, and sell the on the streets for fifteen thousand each, a three-for-one return on their original investment.

For their part, the Salazars were willing to take less than the going rate as middlemen with their eyes on long-term gains. By dumping vast amounts of cheap co-caine in the United States, the street price would go down—way down—undercutting the price set by the other cartels and establishing the Salazars as *the* people in Colombia to do business with.

If the security the Salazar organization offered didn't convince Medellín and Calí, perhaps that would.

The only way they could manage it would be if the new pipeline worked. This test flight would carry only one ton. Braden's C-123 could easily carry twelve times that much, but Roberto was not yet ready to entrust that much to a single flight.

Let Diamond and the CIA pilot prove themselves first. After that, each flight north would carry two hundred million dollars' worth of product or more. The Salazars would corner the coca production markets in South America, and Medellín and Calí would come begging for a piece of the action.

Qué bueno. José finished counting the stacks of money, then nodded to Roberto.

"Well, Señor Braden," the older man said, smiling. "Perhaps you would like to relax for a while. You have time before dinner for a swim."

Braden eyed the girls by the pool and grinned. "You know, Don Roberto, that's the best idea I've heard yet."

"I will go see to the refueling and loading of Señor Braden's aircraft," José said. He left the two men by the pool and started across the lawn toward the garage. He would take one of the jeeps out to the 1,200-meter runway and supervise the operation himself. He wanted to evaluate for himself the people Braden had brought along as assistants on this flight.

There was always a chance that the CIA contract

pilot was still serving his former employers, despite his
recent service to both Diamond and the Salazars. If
there was even a hint of betrayal, Braden and his
people would die . . . unpleasantly. That DEA agent
they'd captured at the summit last week, he'd taken a
long time to die, and *El Tiburón* had learned some new
tricks from the ex-army officer who handled Roberto's
interrogations. Perhaps he would get a chance to try
them out on this smug and offensive gringo.

As José approached the garage he paused, aware of
a new, sweetish odor. It seemed to be coming from inside. The door was open. Stealthily, José slipped into
the building.

Inside were several jeeps and Land Rovers, as well
as two new Mowag Rolands, huge in the semidarkness.
Roberto was proud of the Rolands, chunky, four-
wheeled armored cars with squat turrets mounting .50
caliber machine guns. Roberto had purchased them directly from Mowag of Kreuzlingen in Switzerland, in-
tending to use them to patrol his property along the
north slope of the Sierra Nevadas. Bandits—and rivals
in the drug trade—had been raiding his marijuana
crops there, but the knowledge that a pair of armored
cars were in the area ought to discourage that activity
in short order.

The smell was stronger inside the garage.

Moving swiftly, José stepped around the rear of one
of the Rolands. One of the *pistoleros*, a teenage boy
named Rudy, was leaning against the armored car,
smoking a cigarette laced with *basuco*.

José lashed out with his hand, slapping the cigarette

to the concrete floor, then grinding it beneath his heel. *"Huevón!"* he snapped. "Stupid prick!"

Basuco was a crude cocaine base, similar to the crack cocaine that had already proven so deadly in the United States. Mixed with tobacco and smoked, it was cheap, addictive, and provided an intense high.

It was also usually laced with lead from the gasoline used in its processing. There were side streets in Bogotá and Colombia's other major cities that were home to hundreds of the shambling wrecks who had addicted themselves to *basuco*. Lead poisoning was neither a fast nor a particularly pleasant way to die.

"Hey, fresco, José—" the boy began, a lopsided grin on his face. "Take it easy—"

The *narcotrafficante*'s left hand closed on the soldier's collar, tightening, lifting him against the hard metal of the Roland. His right hand slipped his Beretta from its holster and brought the weapon up to within a centimeter of the kid's nose.

"I am Señor Salazar, *campesino*," José said, his voice filled with a venomous fury. "And you will not smoke that excrement while you work for me. When you were a punk *sicario* on the streets of Medellín, that was one thing. While you work for me, you will have a clear head. *Claro?*"

The kid's eyes crossed as he tried to focus them on the muzzle of the automatic. *"S-si. Claro, señor.* I just . . . I mean, sometimes just for fun . . . Everybody, all my friends—"

José released the kid's collar, then jacked back the slide on the pistol, chambering a round. Holding the muzzle against the kid's upper lip, he fished into his pocket and produced a fifty-peso coin. He put it in the kid's hand. "Toss it."

"Señor?"

He brought the muzzle of the pistol up until it rested squarely between the kid's eyes. "Toss it. Now. Don't drop it."

The coin flashed in the dim light, spinning. The boy caught it, slapping it down on the back of his wrist. His hands were trembling, but somehow he kept from losing it.

"Call it."

The boy was trembling now with almost epileptic fervor. He brought his wrist up, managed to pull his eyes away from the Beretta long enough to focus on the coin trapped under his hand. *"La-las cabezas,"* he stammered. "Heads . . ."

José stood death still for a long moment, enjoying the young *basuco* smoker's terror, enjoying the power that emanated from the gun. He allowed himself a smile. The kid's eyes squeezed shut as the fifty-peso piece clattered onto the floor.

"You live," José said, decocking the weapon at last. *"This* time you live. If I catch you smoking that shit again, however . . ."

"No, sir! I mean, yes sir! I mean, it won't happen again, señor—"

"Get out of here!"

The kid vanished through the garage door. José watched him go, and laughed.

ⓦ Chapter Seven

SECURITY RESTRICTIONS SHARPLY LIMITED flights into the small airfield at Camp Peary. For that reason, Senator Buchanan's helicopter had been routed a few miles down the Peninsula, to a runway at Langley Air Force Base, just outside the cities of Hampton and Newport News. The helicopter touched down at two-thirty Monday afternoon. Weston was there with a limousine and driver, waiting to meet it.

Buchanan stooped beneath the turning rotor blades, hurrying across the tarmac. Weston shook hands with the senator, held the limo's rear door for him, then walked around and got in on the other side.

Ten minutes later, the car left the base on Route 167, passing the NASA buildings and Aerospace Park. Threading the cloverleaf junction with Highway 64, it followed the signs for Williamsburg and Richmond, heading northwest up the Virginia Peninsula.

Weston and Buchanan had a lot to talk about. Since they'd seen each other on Friday, Buchanan had briefed the President and Weston had debriefed Drake.

And it was clearer now than ever that the good guys were losing the war on drugs.

James Weston knew narcotics and narcotics trafficking. Recruited into the CIA thirty-eight years earlier, while he was still a political science major in college, he'd begun his career with the Company, as insiders called it, in the Office of Global Issues. Operated under the Intelligence Directorate, one of the CIA's four major branches, Global Issues analyzed international economic and technological issues, followed the course of foreign commodities and trade, and reported to the DDI—the Deputy Director of Intelligence—on such matters as weapons transfers, international terrorism, and narcotics production.

It was not exactly the flash-bang stuff of spy fiction. For the better part of four decades Weston's career as a spook had been limited to analyzing data from a variety of sources no more clandestine than *Pravda* or Bogotá's *El Espectador*, and compiling reports that might—sometimes—find their way into the National Intelligence Estimate, the CIA's data input into the NSC.

By 1980, though, he was on the staff of the DDI, working in the Office of African and Latin American Analysis. His particular area of expertise was the drug cartels of South America. The eighties were witness to an unprecedented flood of drugs—cocaine especially—entering the United States from South America and Mexico. The pipelines crossed dozens of international boundaries; coca leaves might be grown in Bolivia or Peru, processed in the jungles of Colombia, and shipped north with the connivance of government and military authorities in Panama, Cuba, and the Bahamas. It was Weston's job to trace those pipelines and to assess the importance of the *narcotrafficantes* in the economies of fifteen different nations.

Then, in 1986, he'd been transferred to Project RAMROD. The rumor circulating among his staffers held that someone further up the ladder simply wasn't believing the figures he was turning out on the amount of cocaine entering the States. Two hundred *tons* in 1985 alone? Ridiculous!

In fact, he'd been recruited by Senator Buchanan. Group Seven, the President's new secret narcotics task force, was interested in the possibility of adapting the military's defunct combat robot program for narcotics work, and Weston, with his understanding of the staggering scope of the drug problem, was a logical choice to head the project that, by that time, was being kept alive by CIA funding.

Technically, as RAMROD's project director, Weston no longer worked for the Agency, though he still reported to the DDI. Certainly, his current position was a lot more exciting than reading foreign newspapers or analyzing the economics of coca production in Bolivia.

But his expertise in the drug traffic was proving more valuable than ever now.

"The new CIA figures will be published next week," he told the senator. "Eighty-seven percent of all crime in this country is directly linked to narcotics. From the twelve-year-old who rips off a stereo to feed his crack habit to the Sicilian Mafia, it's the drug trade that's behind them. That *feeds* them. And it's going to get worse."

"That's what I told the President on Saturday," Buchanan said quietly. "I gave him the results of Group

Seven's last study. His staff is already calling it 'the Buchanan Report.' "

Weston's eyebrows rose. "What did the President say?"

"Say? What could he say? My God, look at what we're predicting! Ten to fifteen more years of things going the way they are, and the President and Congress are going to have to suspend the Constitution of the United States! Arrests and searches without warrants, confiscation of all privately owned weapons, martial law, internal travel permits, federal ID cards for every citizen. Narcoterrorism—*here*, in America—on a scale no one in this country has ever dreamed of. Hell, I'm surprised he didn't chuck us out of the White House bodily."

"I can imagine." Weston had been shocked when he'd first heard the conclusions drawn by Group Seven's inner circle. They were *predictions*, not recommendations . . . but there appeared to be no way to escape them. The flood of illegal drugs into the United States was undermining the very foundations of the country. They'd already poisoned the inner cities, where cheap crack and heroin enslaved the weak and the hopeless, where drug gangs fought full-auto gun battles in the streets for control of a few city blocks, and the local dope kings raked in millions.

And the plague was spreading. Two weeks earlier, there'd been a firefight between members of a white motorcycle gang and a Jamaican posse in the streets of Baezley, Pennsylvania, population 8,296. Twelve people were dead and seventeen wounded; five of the deaths had been innocent passersby caught in the cross-fire.

Collateral damage.

Twenty-seven police departments that Weston knew of were currently under Federal investigation, facing charges of corruption, bribery, and narcotics trafficking. The departments represented cities and towns with populations ranging from over one million down to 1,348, and those twenty-seven were only the tip of the iceberg. The corruption was thought to have touched hundreds of state senators and representatives, dozens of mayors, thousands of government officials, and at least three governors. And it didn't stop with the state governments. Eighteen members of the U.S. House of Representatives, four U.S. senators, and hundreds of lawyers, lobbyists, aides, and other political figures were suspected of accepting money—disguised as campaign contributions, reelection funds, or private reimbursements—from organizations fronting for individuals ranging from street-corner pushers to Fabio Ochoa.

The corruption, the *rot* seemed to be everywhere.

Suggested courses of action ranged from invading Colombia to legalizing drugs. No one seriously wanted a war in South America that would make Vietnam seem like a skirmish by comparison. As for legalization, Group Seven's study had concluded that legal drugs would only accelerate the cancer while doing little or nothing to stop the criminal elements who were battling for control of the American drug market.

It seemed unthinkable, but in ten more years, fifteen

at the most, Americans might well be living under what could only be described as a military dictatorship.

It would be that, or total anarchy. There were no other choices.

"We discussed RAMROD," Buchanan said. "The President is interested in the possibility of using him in the field."

"That won't be enough," Weston warned. "Not by itself."

"Hell, I know that. But we've got to start someplace."

"Biggest problem now is Chris Drake," Weston said. "We *need* him if RAMROD is going to be tested in the field. No one else has worked as well with the robot as he has. I swear, the two of them think alike. It will take months to train someone else."

"Poor bastard. His wife and daughter, raped and murdered in their own home," Buchanan said. "How is he?"

"Not . . . good. He was forced into a position where he had to act . . . or be murdered, along with his wife and kid. He acted, did the best he could, and his people were killed anyway, right in front of his eyes. When the police broke in, they found him sitting on that bed, the muzzle of a pistol in his mouth."

"Oh God." Buchanan digested that a moment. "The press is having a field day with this, you know. The sanctity of home and family violated, brutalized by street-gang dopers . . ."

"They're also speculating that Chris was dealing on the side," Weston said. "That he had a stash inside his house and a biker gang ripped him off because he was dealing on their turf."

"He wasn't, was he?"

"Hell no. Somebody went to a lot of trouble to make it look that way, though."

"My God, why?"

Weston took a deep breath. "Obviously, because he survived SNOWDROP."

"But why the charade with the biker gang, the cocaine planted in his house—"

"Not to mention a submachine gun that's been matched ballistically to a gang drug hit in Richmond last week. My guess is that someone figured that if Drake was murdered by himself, we'd know someone wanted him silenced. But if he and his family were the victims of a drug rip-off or random gang violence, well . . . we might suspect, but we'd never know."

"Do you think they know he's alive?"

"I hope not. I tried to foster the idea that he was killed. I thought it might be safer that way . . . for him. And for us."

"How'd you manage that?"

"We got lucky. Some of the neighbors heard automatic weapons fire and called the police. They were on the scene pretty fast and managed to talk Chris down, stop him from pulling the trigger. Because of his classified work, he was carrying one of those in-case-of-emergency-call numbers. The cops called it and got me. So I arranged with the cops to take charge of him."

"The police are cooperating then?"

"Yeah. I just trotted out 'matter of national security' and waved my CIA card. They went along with it."

"So you have him safe?"

"At the Farm." Weston sighed. "I couldn't even let him go to the funeral today. *Three* caskets, incidentally, just in case someone was keeping count. Like Diamond."

"Mmm. Group Seven went over your report yesterday, James," Buchanan said. "I should tell you, not everyone accepts your analysis. This . . . Diamond, a name Drake overheard. There's nothing to link him with Colombia. He could be some small-time, local dealer."

"Bull," Weston replied. "The SNOWDROP team was ambushed by forces working with the Salazars. American assets, probably CIA contract mercenaries, were involved. Four days later, the day after he gets back, the one survivor is assaulted in his own home. And leading the bad guys is none other than the guy who was the SEALs' DEA liaison in Colombia . . . supposedly dead."

"Emilio Esposito."

Weston nodded. "When I debriefed Drake on Saturday, I took along Esposito's DEA file. He looked at the file photo and told me that it was *not* the Esposito he knew."

Buchanan looked at Weston, startled. "I hadn't heard that."

"I thought it best not to broadcast it. It means the real Emilio Esposito was hit somewhere between Bogotá and the SEALs' drop zone. This whole thing is too tightly organized, too big to be run by some local pusher. What we've seen so far spells organization to me, Senator. Big organization. And big money."

"Could Diamond be DEA? Someone working with the false Esposito?"

Weston shook his head. "Nope. CIA."

"Christ, James! You're not serious!"

"I'm afraid I've never been more serious. This affair has Agency written all over it. Whoever is behind it all is able to jigger schedules, deploy CIA helo and contract mercenary assets, even get at Agency records."

"What records?"

"I went up to Langley yesterday and did some checking in their files." He was referring to the CIA headquarters near McLean, Virginia, just inside the Capital Beltway, rather than the Air Force base they'd just left. "The evening he got back from Colombia, Drake was debriefed by two Company men. I looked up their report."

"And?"

"It was classified F-5."

"But that means—"

"That it'll be buried. Correct."

Standard practice assigned CIA intelligence reports a letter-number combination that evaluated their reliability. The letters graded the source, from "A," meaning completely reliable, to "E"—unreliable—and "F"—reliability unknown. By giving Drake an F, someone at Langley was saying they had no way of judging how good a source he was. The numbers, which assessed the reliability of the source's information, ran from "1," for information already confirmed by other sources, to "5," improbable, and "6," reliability cannot be determined.

An evaluation of F-5 meant Drake's debriefing report

would be given little weight, even though his eyewitness account of the ambush suggested that there was an intelligence leak in Washington.

"So you assume that Diamond is CIA because he had access to the SNOWDROP debriefing. He gave it a low reliability rating so that no one would pay attention to it."

"It seems the likeliest explanation, sir. That debriefing strongly suggested Agency complicity. SNOWDROP was supposed to be picked up by an unmarked helo flown by a CIA contract pilot named Braden. Instead—"

"The helo was full of troops."

"Probably contract mercs out of Central America. We're checking on that. But it all points to someone up at Langley."

"What the hell is going on over there?" the senator demanded. "Hitting our own people! And I thought CIA policy specifically prohibited having anything to do with narcotics!"

"It does. But remember, everything over there is compartmented for security's sake. Directors don't always know what's going on in their own department. We could be looking at a rogue operation. Someone in the CIA chain of command has gone into business for himself. Someone in a position to tap Company field assets."

"Christ, James! We've got to get this guy! The CIA is already thoroughly involved both with Group Seven and with RAMROD. If Diamond is in on Group Seven planning, he'll pass everything to his buddies in Colombia!"

"The thought had crossed my mind," Weston said dryly.

The limousine left 64, swinging onto the desolate stretch of road that led to Camp Peary's front gate. Both men began fishing for their wallets. The guards would want to see their IDs.

What worried Weston was the fact that Esposito— the fake Esposito—had risked showing himself. That they'd gone to such trouble to eliminate Drake—and in a way designed to both discredit him and avoid suspicion that he'd been deliberately silenced—meant that the man masquerading as Esposito was going to be used again, presumably someplace where Drake might have recognized him.

But where? How did he fit in with Diamond?

And did Diamond know that Drake had not been silenced, after all?

Weston feared it was only a matter of time before Diamond knew that the SEAL lieutenant was alive.

And when he did, he would strike again.

His survival depended on it.

Drake lay in his cot, in a gray-walled room with a guard outside his door.

The room was part of the Camp Peary dispensary. His chart listed him as under observation.

Under observation was right. A wire-protected TV lens watched him from high in one corner. The doctors were afraid he'd try to kill himself again.

He closed his eyes. He'd been so close. So *close.* The gun, the Walther PPK he'd bought Meagan years ago as protection for when he was away, had been in the drawer of her bedside table. It hadn't helped her. She'd obviously not been able to reach it when the thugs broke in.

Probably they'd grabbed her when she answered the door. Maybe they'd posed as telephone repairmen.

Damn, damn, damn! He remembered his despair when he opened the drawer and saw the gun lying there. He remembered the gunpowder-metal taste as he'd placed the muzzle in his mouth, remembered the numb bitterness as he sat on the bed, surrounded by death . . . *death*. . . .

Why hadn't he been able to pull the trigger when the police burst in?

The evening's events continued to recycle themselves in his mind: his crawl toward the preoccupied guard, his race toward the bedroom, the unexpected appearance of Julio. He'd been over the situation time after time after time. What else could he have done? *What else could he have done?*

He'd had two and only two choices: do nothing and be slaughtered like a trussed-up sheep along with Meagan and Stacy, or rush into the room in the hope of catching their captors off guard.

But the unpredictable had happened and he'd lost the element of surprise. One of the bad guys had picked up a gun.

And Stacy and Meagan were dead. He'd failed them. He could not see past that single fact. Their lives had depended on *him* . . . and he'd failed them.

Why hadn't he been able to join them? *Why?*

There was a knock, and then the door opened. Weston walked in, followed by someone familiar. Who was it? Yes . . . Senator Buchanan.

"Hello, son," Weston said. "How are you doing?"

Drake turned his head back toward the window, unwilling to look at them, unwilling to talk.

"Lieutenant," the senator said, coming closer. "I was terribly sorry to hear about your family. Please accept my . . . my most sincere condolences. I know what you must be going through."

"Right." The word was sharply bitten off, raw in his throat.

"I hope you don't mind, Chris," Weston said. "I brought the senator along because I thought . . . well, I thought he might be able to convince you."

"I can't do what you're asking me," Drake said. He fought the burning in his eyes. "I *can't*. . . ."

He knew what Weston wanted. RAMROD's director had suggested it Saturday, when he'd come to question Drake about what had happened.

"You saw those men," Weston said. "You could help us identify them. And if we nail them, they can lead us to Diamond."

Drake shook his head. "I told you what I could. I gave you their descriptions."

"A tall, Latin-looking guy named Luis? A shorter, blond-haired man with a Texan accent? Those descriptions could be anybody, Chris," Weston said. "But there's another way—"

"I told you, no." Drake squeezed his eyes shut, trying to close out his visitors, the pain. He didn't *want* to remember.

Buchanan's hand touched his shoulder. "I meant

what I said earlier," he said. "I know what you're going through."

"You know." Anger flared. Drake rose from the cot, his fist clenched. "You know!"

"Yes, damn it," Buchanan snapped, pulling back his hand. "You're not the only one whose life has been ruined by this . . . this *curse!*"

"That's easy for you to say, you sanctimonious son of a—"

"You think so? Talk to my wife. Ask *her* what it's like to have your only son killed. By drugs!"

Buchanan's words were biting, sharp. Drake's eyes locked with his.

"Your son . . ."

"Five years ago. It took him four hours to die after a head-on collision that killed two other people and left a sixteen-year-old girl in a coma for life. And you want to know the hell of it? The whole affair was hushed up. 'Senator's Son Dead in Highway Crash.' That's how the headlines read. What my staff covered up was the fact that Mike was the driver, that he admitted to the police he'd been flying on coke at a party that evening. It was *his* fault that three people died and others had their lives ruined. His fault . . . and mine."

"Yours . . . sir?"

"Mine." Buchanan turned away. "Oh, you know all the hoary clichés. If I'd been around more. If Mike hadn't had things so easy. God knows being a politician's son is never easy, but he had money and a car and a taste for a swinging life style. Yeah, I blame myself. So does my wife. The only thing keeping us together now is the damned job. Senators *don't* get divorces."

Drake wanted to say something but held his tongue. He could see where the obvious and banal rejoinder— "it wasn't your fault"—would come boomeranging back at him.

And yes, it was true. Could he really blame himself for the fact that Meagan and Stacy were dead? Any more than Buchanan could blame himself for the death of his son?

Drake slumped back down to the cot. "There's . . . nothing I can do." He could feel the fear, ice-cold and dark. He didn't want to look at it, couldn't face it. . . .

"You can *fight*, damn it," Buchanan said. "What happened to my son nearly killed me. But I'm fighting back." He paused. "You're cleared for Group Seven, aren't you? You know what it is?"

"Yes, sir."

"Well, Group Seven's *my* way of striking back at the bastards. I *built* it, back when the Reagan administration first proposed the idea. That was the year after Mike died." He stopped, his Adam's apple bobbing as he swallowed. "Group Seven," he continued after a moment, "was designed to find ways to combat the drug problem. New ways . . . innovative ways, because the old ways haven't been working. You're already a part of one of our projects."

"RAMROD."

"Right. We need you, son. If you quit now, you've just given the sons of bitches an easy victory."

"He's right," Weston added. "On the way down here, we were talking about how bad things are getting.

Crime. Firefights in the streets. Things happening to ordinary, decent people . . . like what happened to you. It's getting worse, and if we don't do something soon, this country is going to look like downtown Beirut in less time than I care to think about."

Buchanan's fists clenched at his side, white-knuckled, working. "Lieutenant, I'll be *damned* if I'll just sit back and watch these drug lord bastards buy, steal, corrupt, or drug my country into ruin! What we're asking you, son, is that you help us. Maybe it's too late to help your family. But you can still help yourself. You can help us!"

He thought about it. The fear was still there . . . mingled with the mindless grief.

But there was another emotion as well, one he'd not recognized before.

Hatred.

Until he became a SEAL, Drake had never thought much about drug lords or their product. Even when he'd been shipped off to Colombia on SNOWDROP, they'd been abstractions, targets, creatures of adventure fiction and "Miami Vice" reruns.

Yet somehow, those men, those bloated monsters in their multimillion-dollar palaces and penthouses and yachts, had reached out and, with less thought than they'd give to crushing a fly, had wiped his family off the face of the earth.

He found he hated these faceless beings, these less-than-human leeches who thrived on the weakness and miseries and deaths of people.

No more. *No more!* He wanted to strike back. He *had*

to strike back to win some measure of peace for Meagan and Stacy.

And for himself.

"I'll help if I can," he said quietly. He saw a tightness in Weston's face relax.

"I knew you'd come through, son," the CIA man said.

"I still don't know . . . if I can . . ."

"We'll take it a step at a time, son. Dr. McDaniels knows what she's doing. I've discussed it with her, and it should be safe enough."

But Drake didn't care about safe.

It was the memories, *facing* the memories, that he feared.

◔ *Chapter Eight*

AN HOUR LATER, Drake was back in Lab One as McDaniels and Costrini and Irvin and the rest pumped his hand and asked how he was and told him how sorry they were. Drake managed to tell them that he was fine . . . managed, too, to ignore the sad, pitying looks he caught out of the corner of his eye.

Strangely, he was, if not fine, at least . . . handling the grief, and for now that was enough. Once he'd made up his mind to act, he found he was able to move, to think . . . where he'd thought he never wanted to move again.

Hatred, he discovered, was a source of tremendous strength.

"Hello, Lieutenant Drake," a familiar, almost cultured baritone voice said. "I understand that you wish to try something different this afternoon."

Drake turned and was surprised to see Rod dressed in civilian clothes. He was used to seeing the robot either without clothing or with the utilitarian combat blacks worn by men going through Kiddie Land. This . . . man looked like any casually dressed American, in blue jeans, slip-on deck shoes, and a colorful madras sport shirt.

"It's Weston's idea, Rod," he replied. "I don't know if I'm ready for this or not."

"Actually," McDaniels said, "it was my idea. And Chris . . . I don't want you to even think about going through with it if you're not a hundred-percent sure. I know . . . I know what it must be costing you."

Drake shook his head. "Don't talk me out of it. Let's *do* it." He looked at Rod as he settled himself into a chair. "Are *you* ready for this?"

"I am. The idea is . . . interesting. I do not believe anything of this kind has been attempted before. However, it should work in principle, with CORA's help, of course."

One of the technicians was already pulling Rod's shirttail up and working the end of a cable into the robot's receptor.

McDaniels brought him a PARET helmet. "Chris," she said. "I want you to think carefully about what you're doing. You've had a . . . a bad time, and—"

He took the helmet from her and put it on. "Run it," he said. "I want these people, and if pulling them out of my head is the only way to get them, that's what we're going to do."

"Printer on," CORA's voice said out of the air. A large, boxy gray machine like a photocopier clicked and hummed on a bench in the corner of the lab. "Direct access," CORA continued. "Initiating . . ."

"If this works," Weston said from nearby, "we're about to revolutionize the science of criminology."

The laser printer was kept hooked to the computer

system strung through Lab One for those times when the technicians needed a sheet of hardcopy, especially when they needed to scrutinize a schematic diagram of some piece of circuitry in Rod's innards. Printed schematics were easier to read than glowing lines on a TV monitor.

Computers work with pictures, any pictures, by scanning the image and digitizing it, which means reducing it to a pattern of dots stored as numbers in the computer's memory. As with photographs printed in a newspaper, the image can be reproduced by a printer that can read those numbers and recreate the dots. The laser printer was capable of exceptionally fine resolution.

The key to Dr. McDaniels's idea was the knowledge that the final picture was the product of numbers, *only* numbers.

And it didn't matter at all where those numbers came from.

Teeth set, eyes closed, Drake remembered driving up to the house, walking up to the door, stepping inside. . . .

Pain . . . and the horror of an unexpected attack . . . helplessness . . .

Esposito smiling, too far away to reach.

"Hey, boss! When does the fun start?"

And later . . .

"God, Chris!" Meagan's face, terrified. "Oh God, Chris! Who are these people? You . . . you know one of them?"

"Yeah, I know him."

"But who is he? Where did you——"

"Look, honey, if you don't know, maybe I can convince

them to let you go. So no questions, okay? Just stay calm. It'll be all right."

And later still . . .

"*Listen, guy. Nothing personal, okay?*"

"*You son-of-a-bitch bastard!*"

"*Hey! C'mon, Luis! Let's haul ass, for Chrissakes! Diamond doesn't want us anywhere around when this goes down, okay?*"

"*Go on, then! Anyway, Lieutenant, sorry it had to be like this. Just business, you know?*"

Weston hurried toward the chair where Drake sat, face taut in a hideous, teeth-baring rictus, fists clenched on the countertop before him so tightly they shook, white-knuckled, rigidly locked.

"What is it?" Weston called. "What's wrong?"

The robot, standing impassively a few feet away, swayed suddenly, then crashed to the floor. McDaniels, snapping orders, stooped next to the robot's body, which was twitching now as though suspended on the brink of an epileptic seizure. Its eyes were wide open, staring at the fluorescent lighting fixtures on the ceiling. "CORA!" McDaniels screamed. She was trying to hold the trembling robot, trying to pull it to her. "Discontinue access! Discontinue access!"

"Unable to comply . . ."

Tears streamed down McDaniels's face. Rod twitched and shuddered in her arms.

"*Listen, guy. Nothing personal, okay?*"

Running down the hall. Obscene, grunting noises, sounds of lust . . . sickening . . .

If he could just catch them unarmed. Their only chance . . .

"Whee-oo! Hey, Arturo! Get the fuck in here and have some!" The door banging open . . . Julio striding through . . . "These honeys are sweet!"

Gunfire, shredding Julio's shirt and chest, a savage, thundering burst . . .

Rod had never felt anything like it before, an inner pang of loneliness and grief and loss and empty yearning. Properly speaking, he had never *felt* anything, ever, but the distinction was a minor one.

God, I'll kill them! I've got to save Meagan and Stacy!

Gunfire and horror . . . obscene movements in nightmare shadows . . .

No! *Denial and rage in a room painted with blood . . . blood!*

With the horror came pain. Servo relays in Rod's legs and arms fired randomly, wracking his body with convulsions.

Override! Override! Reestablish autonomous control. . . .

Meagan! Stacy! No!

His optical feed circuits had tripped out. His eyes were open, but visual was out. He restored the circuit and sight returned, harsh at first, until he adjusted for the room's fluorescent lighting. He seemed to be lying on his back, his head cradled in Dr. McDaniels's arms.

How had that happened?

Rod ran a diagnostic on his own systems, checking autonomic responses and on-line programming. Everything was functioning within normal parameters.

Yet *something* had happened, even though Rod wasn't sure what.

Gently, he disentangled himself from Dr. McDaniels. "Rod!" she said. Her face was wet. "Are you okay?"

"Function nominal," he replied. Rising, he looked around the room. Drake was removing the PARET helmet, Weston anxiously helping him.

"Chris! What the hell happened?" The CIA man looked from the SEAL to Rod and back again.

"I'm okay, I'm okay!" Drake said. His face, too, was wet. "Damn, I'm sorry. My fault. I guess I kind of lost control."

Rod's acute senses detected Drake's increased heart rate, the flushed skin, the tension in his voice. He was upset, but otherwise he seemed functional.

"What do you mean, Chris?" McDaniels asked. "Lost control how?"

"I was . . . remembering." Drake's hands clenched again, then slowly relaxed. Rod could see that they were trembling, ever so slightly. "Good God, it was like I was *there* again. I couldn't handle it."

"Damn!" McDaniels said. "I was afraid of that. A feedback loop . . ."

Weston shook his head. "Feedback what?"

The PARET helmet worked by generating a weak electromagnetic field that registered the neural patterns of the subject. It also tended to isolate those patterns, insulating them from distracting thoughts or outside interference. That had very much the same effect in humans as a light hypnotic trance, the sort that allowed a human to remember things in vivid detail, even if they had happened years before.

And sometimes there was the faintest echo, reinforcing those patterns, strengthening them. Rod understood the phenomena perfectly, even though it was poorly understood in human PARET subjects. In computers it was called a programming loop.

Fascinating that it could happen in humans as well.

He could still feel the effects of a similar loop within his own thought processes. Strange . . . his memory was perfect, but that black, sinking, nightmarish sense of loss he'd experienced for a moment was fading. Already he found it impossible to recapture it, even to recall it.

But something had happened, hadn't it? *Something* had changed.

No. All systems were functioning nominally.

An inner command superimposed a window on his visual display. The faces of two men, drawn from Drake's memory, stared back at him within his own mind, and he felt an inner shiver of . . . what? Fear . . . anger . . . loathing . . .

Could a robot . . . *hate*?

"Mr. Weston," Rod said. "I have the information you required. It is coming through on the printer now."

The laser printer in the corner began to hum as paper fed into the machine.

They were photographs, halftones indistinguishable from the black-and-white portraits that might have been printed in a magazine. Rod watched impassively as Drake, Weston, and McDaniels looked at the photos. Others crowded around, fascinated by what were, in effect, snapshots of a man's memories.

McDaniels suddenly looked up. "Wait a minute! All

of you . . . out!" She began herding the other RAMROD technicians away.

"What's the matter, Doctor?" Weston asked.

"Good God, Mr. Weston! You realize what we're looking at there? Surely Chris has a right to *some* privacy. . . ."

Rod had trouble understanding the concept, but he saw Weston nod. "Maybe we should clear the room. Chris?"

"Sure. Whatever you want." He sounded tired, weak. "Heather can stay, if she wants. . . ."

Weston looked at McDaniels. "Okay, everybody out," he said quietly. "You can stay, Doctor. But I think we'd better keep this to the three of us for the moment." His eyes met Rod's for an instant. "The *four* of us."

Four of the photos showed the four murderers in Drake's home, each captured at a different moment, their expressions showing various emotions: surprise, pain, anger, lust. They seemed exaggerated, and Rod wondered if they really had looked like that, or if their expressions had been exaggerated by Drake's memory. The last two were of Esposito and the blond man who had brought the MAC-10.

Weston pointed to one. "Well, we know that's not Esposito. Not the real one, anyway."

"Right."

Rod's head cocked slightly to one side, a human mannerism he was still learning to imitate. Somewhere at the back of his mind, separated from that part of his brain used to communicate with the humans, images—photographs stored in literally millions of electronic files—flickered at the edge of awareness. "I am now scanning police and government records for all subjects," he said. "I have positive matches for the four dead men. Hardcopy briefs are coming through now."

The printer hummed. Weston reached into the output hopper and removed three pages. "Yep," he said. "These are the names the police came up with at the time. Federico Chaco Vegas. His brother Julio. Arturo Alvarez, Ramón Gomez. All street-level hoods. Members of a Hispanic gang called *Los Salvajes.* Long arrest records, all of them . . . possession . . . distribution . . ."

Drake reached out and took one of the sheets. "Chaco Vegas," he said. His voice was brittle, like ice. "He's the one . . ."

"He's dead, son," Weston said. "You killed him."

"I remember." Drake seemed to shake himself, then looked sharply at Rod. "Look at the heading on these files! These are Virginia State Police arrest records! He's pulling them out of Richmond somehow, and printing them here!"

"I have completed examining the computer files for state and local police in Virginia, Maryland, the District of Columbia, and the Portsmouth-Norfolk-Virginia Beach area," Rod said. "I have now accessed the computer files of the FBI in Washington, D.C."

Drake's eyes widened. "My God! Can he *do* that?"

McDaniels shrugged. Her eyes had scarcely left Rod since his fall, and she still looked worried. "Rod has a built-in cellular phone system," she explained. "And an internal modem. If he knew the number and the passwords, I guess he could tap into any computer system anywhere, as long as it had a modem hookup, too."

"Acquiring the appropriate numbers is simply a matter of accessing the appropriate electronic directories," Rod said. Images continued to flicker through some remote part of his awareness. "The passwords are more difficult, but since the files are designed for broad-based official user access, they are generally available in help menus or police files."

"God damn," Drake said. "You people have created a robot hacker!"

Weston was watching Rod intently. "Good intelligence is the key to any war," he said. "Maybe Rod's best weapon in the war on drugs will be *information*."

Rod continued to run through the FBI files. They were enormous, far larger and more comprehensive than the police files. He narrowed his search to East Coast records compiled within the past five years.

The images of the two unknown men remained in his mind as the records blurred past. Smiling. *Evil*. Rod had known the dictionary definition of the word *evil* but had not been certain that he felt what it meant.

Looking at those two faces in his memory—in *Drake's* memory—somehow explained the word.

There was a satisfying inner click of resolution in the back of Rod's mind. "I have another match," he said. He activated the printer again. "Hardcopy is coming through now."

Weston picked up the data sheet and rapidly scanned it. "It's our blond friend. Oh, shit . . ." He looked up at Drake. "Our old friend Michael Howard Braden."

"The helo pilot . . ." Drake's face was grim.

Weston kept reading for a moment, more carefully now. *"Shit!"* he said. "This is a 201 file."

"What's that?" McDaniels wanted to know.

"It means the guy's worked for the CIA. We've got a live one here."

"Indications are that the subject escaped by motor vehicle," Rod said. "There is no record of his death with—"

McDaniels laid a hand on Rod's arm. "That's not what he meant, Rod," she said.

Weston held up the printout and read aloud. "Michael Howard Braden. Born Dallas, 1947. West Dallas High . . . Texas A&M . . . Here we are. Served with Special Operations Group beginning 1969. Helicopter pilot . . . and fixed-wing transports. Flew special missions for the CIA into Laos and Cambodia in the early seventies. Discharged in '74. Looks like he maintained Company contacts, though. He was a contract pilot in Nicaragua starting in '76, first with the *Somozistas*, later with the Contras." Weston looked up. "He's still listed on the 201 as a CIA contract agent."

"What does that mean?" McDaniels asked.

"Means he's a freelancer, working for the Company part-time. And according to this, he's on active status now."

"In the hospital in Panama with dysentery," Drake said, his voice tightly controlled. "My ass. He was there, with Esposito. Does that mean this is all CIA?"

"A rogue operation," Weston said. He shook his head. "God, a rogue op. It proves Diamond is Company, because only a Company man could pull something like this together. And it means Diamond has other Company people working for him."

"The same voice," Drake said, remembering. "The

same accent. Braden flew that helo dust-off in Colombia. But instead of a rescue—"

"He set you up. It fits."

"It might also give us a handle on Diamond," Drake said. "Braden's got to know how to contact him. Maybe he even knows the guy. . . ."

Weston looked at Rod. "There's no address listed here. What else can you get on the bastard?"

"Checking."

"Unfortunately," Weston said, "Rod's only going to be able to work with information that's part of the system. He caught Braden because the guy was stupid enough to show his face at Chris's house."

"Not stupid," Drake said. "I was as good as dead. I think—"

"I have additional information," Rod said. He was expanding his search of government files, hunting for the man who had impersonated the real Esposito, still with no success. But he'd turned up something relevant on Braden.

"Whatcha got, son?" Weston asked.

"Item. Michael Braden is still listed as being in Gorgas Army Hospital, Panama. However, the Gorgas patient records show no one there by that name.

"Item. A Captain Brady Howard is listed on an Army flight from Bogotá to Andrews Air Force Base yesterday, with a fueling stop at Homestead Air Force Base, Florida.

"And 'Brady Howard' is listed as a cover name for Michael Howard Braden," Weston said, reading the 201-file printout again. "Right."

"That is correct," Rod said. "Item. Agency records

show a CIA safe house in Georgetown being assigned to Michael Beasely three days ago."

"Another cover name." Weston lowered the printout. "This guy gets around, doesn't he?"

"There is a high probability that Braden-Howard-Beasely is currently using the Georgetown safe house as a base of operations," Rod said. "Surveillance or apprehension at that address is a definite possibility."

"You're damned right it's a possibility," Drake said. He looked at Weston, fire in his eyes. "Let's go pick him up."

"Hold on there, son," the CIA man said. "We're not authorized to——"

"The hell with authorization, man," Drake exploded. "What do you want to do, ask permission from your buddies at Langley? Maybe ask Diamond himself?"

"No. Certainly not." Weston looked at Rod again. "I am wondering if we can't use this somehow. Maybe to smoke Diamond out."

"You mean let them know at Langley that we're going after Braden and see who jumps?"

"Something like that." He continued to stare at Rod. "And maybe our friend Rod here is about to get his first field test."

"That would be gratifying," Rod said. "I have long theorized about conditions in the world outside the walls of this facility and have anticipated witnessing them at first hand."

"Whoa, there," Drake said. "You mean you've never been outside the laboratory?"

"Correct," Rod replied. "However, I anticipate no problems in such an operation. My programming has been designed to allow me to function adequately in uncontrolled environments."

McDaniels patted Rod's shoulder. "You may have a few things to learn yet."

"Yeah," Drake said softly. "It's a nasty world out there."

Briefly, Rod wondered how the objective reality of the world outside the lab walls could be different from that inside . . . or from the world he experienced indirectly through the PARET feed. He did not understand but decided that travel outside those walls might well give him the data he needed to resolve the question.

He felt the familiar, satisfying click of numbers matching. "I have a match on the final subject," he said. "Hardcopy is coming through."

Weston picked up the sheet and started reading. "State Department . . . My God, Rod, where did you get this?"

"State Department records on foreign nationals traveling inside the United States," Rod replied. "I could find no sign of the subject in CIA files. However, a newspaper clipping which was scanned and stored with CIA archival material caught my notice and led me to check the appropriate State Department files."

"Colonel Luis Delgado-Valasquez," Weston read. "Colombian national. First entered the U.S. in 1984 as a military attaché with the Colombian embassy. Senior officer believed operating with the DAS."

"DAS?" McDaniels asked. "What's that?"

"Their FBI," Weston replied. "And I think I see now why they were so eager to silence you, Chris."

"Why?"

"Group Seven has been trying to expand our information exchanges with the DAS. I know for a fact this Delgado was slated to work with Group Seven personnel on upcoming joint projects." He shook his head. "Diamond must have figured there was a good chance that you'd run into Delgado. If you did . . ."

"I'd remember him as the guy who led my team into an ambush. Right."

Weston reached into the printer basket. "Here's a copy of that newspaper clipping. And a translation. The original is in Spanish."

"Read it."

"*El Espectador*, 12 November 1986," Weston read. " 'President Barco meets with American diplomats to discuss extradition treaty.' " He compared the photo, which showed the U.S. ambassador shaking hands with Colombian President Virgilio Barco Vargas, with the image taken from Drake's memories.

"Delgado is in the background," Rod said. He extended a hand, pointing to a member of the crowd watching the meeting in the newspaper shot. The figure was wearing a uniform and dark glasses, but the resemblance was unmistakable.

"So I see." Weston returned to the printed biography. "It doesn't say anything here about him working with the drug lords. In fact, he was in charge of government operations against the Medellín cartel in 1988. He led a series of raids that bagged five high-level Medellín people."

"Working against the competition," McDaniels suggested.

"An excellent working hypothesis, Doctor," Rod put

in. "He could well have been working for the Cali cartel."

"Or the Salazars," Weston said. "Yeah. It fits."

"So how do we find him?" Drake asked. "And I do
mean *we*. I'm in on this, Weston. I want this guy."

"You're in," Weston said softly. "As to the how, we
follow up the leads we have." He slapped one of the
dossier printouts on the table. "We start by paying Mr.
Braden a visit."

Rod felt an inner thrill similar to the click of resolution over a satisfactorily completed problem. The sensa-
tion—of satisfaction, of *completion*—was a new one,
which itself was . . . satisfying.

He had already deduced that apprehending Braden
would be the next step in a plan to ferret out Diamond.

He was pleased that Weston was in agreement.

Three hours later, Charles Wilson Vanecki made a
notation in the phone log in the RAMROD telephone
exchange, listing the caller, the number called, and the
time. Vanecki had worked at Langley before the man
he knew as Diamond arranged for his transfer to the
Farm.

Noting that the caller was one of several names he
was paid to take note of, he listened in on the conversation for several moments before another call forced him
to attend to his legal duties.

And hours later, at a service station phone booth outside of Barlowe Corners, Virginia, he made another call
to a memorized phone number that was to be used only
in an emergency. . . .

ⓦ *Chapter Nine*

DRAKE LEANED BACK in the right-hand rear seat of the limousine as it pulled out of Washington National Airport and merged with the traffic heading north on the George Washington Memorial Parkway. Weston sat in the middle, with Rod to his left. The front seat was occupied by the driver and an FBI man named Kenzie, both wearing conservative business suits. Drake had glimpsed an H&K MP5 submachine gun on the floor by Kenzie's foot, and he knew that the driver was armed as well.

Their car was sandwiched between two identical black limos, each of which carried four more armed men.

The ten-man security unit was FBI. Four of them—Kenzie, the driver, and two men in the lead car—were regular agents, but the rest were members of the Federal Bureau of Investigation's elite Hostage Response Team. The HRT—pronounced "Hurt" and sometimes referred to by insiders as "Super-SWAT"—was a fifty-man unit trained in close-quarters combat, special entry techniques, assault tactics, and other standard antiterrorist and hostage-rescue skills. Weston had called

Washington and arranged for the HRT detail to join
the RAMROD party on the Washington National runway reserved for occasional military or official traffic.

"Are they for our protection or to arrest Braden?"
Drake had asked as they climbed out of the Huey and
hurried across the runway to where the three black
limos and their armed escort were waiting.

"A little of both," Weston had replied. "The CIA
doesn't have powers of arrest. That's the FBI's department, which is why I brought them in on this." Weston
had grinned. "Anyway, a few extra guns won't hurt
when we confront our Texan friend, right? We don't
know who he has in there with him, or how well armed
they might be."

The SEAL had been turning the questions over in
his head ever since they'd left the airport. Their escort
was not dressed in the usual SWAT or HRT fashion,
in combat blacks or camouflage fatigues. Instead they
wore conservative business suits, white shirts, and ties,
and seemed uncomfortably out of place.

Drake was uncomfortable, too. Weston had admitted
that there was a possibility Braden would put up a fight
when he was cornered at the CIA's Georgetown safe
house, but he'd refused when Drake asked if he could
carry a weapon. "Only the FBI agents will be armed,"
he said. "Our Bureau friends are, ah, less than enthusi-
astic about people running around D.C. with loaded
weapons."

. So Drake, Weston, and Rod would be unarmed.

If only all of them weren't crowded together into
three cars. Tactically, Drake felt like a sitting duck. He
remembered Weston talking about drawing Diamond

into the open and decided that this must be a part of it. Sure, give the guy a target he couldn't refuse and shoot him before he could spring an ambush.

No problem.

Drake looked out the right-hand window. East, across the river, he could see the marble columns of the Lincoln Memorial at the head of the Arlington Memorial Bridge, and beyond, the sky-piercing thrust of the Washington Monument.

Washington, Drake thought, the tourist's Washington, had always struck him as such a clean city, with its monuments and orderly, parklike streets around the Mall, the splendor of its public buildings, the color of its hordes of out-of-town visitors.

He knew that the tourist's view of the city was quite different from the reality. He'd heard the figures, read the news stories of how drugs were sold openly on street corners within half a mile of the Capitol Building, of how whole neighborhoods lived in a virtual state of siege as rival drug gangs battled with automatic weapons for control of the city's streets.

Drake had never paid much attention to those stories before. His own experiences with the city of Washington had always been limited to the public buildings, the monuments, and the tourists. His favorite place was the Smithsonian Air and Space Museum, where the technological achievements of the past century were on display. It was a bright, clean place of hope and pride far removed from the festering crime and blood of the streets only a few blocks beyond the Mall.

He was seeing the cityscape differently now, as though through different eyes. The drug war was a daily fact of life for the vast majority of the people living there among the brownstones, tenements, and public-housing projects beyond the marble gleam of the government buildings.

Different eyes . . .

He turned away and looked at Rod. How did he see the city? The RAMROD robot appeared to be taking in the passing scenery with its usual passive acceptance. Traffic was picking up as the convoy threaded its way off the parkway close by the Marine Corps Memorial, then entered the suburb of Rosslyn. Futuristic towers of white stone, steel, and glass rose among the expressways, in high-tech contrast to the lower, more classical architecture across the river. Ahead, Drake could see the Francis Scott Key Bridge thrusting across the Potomac into Georgetown. The majestic brown towers of Georgetown University crowned the low hill to the left. Everywhere there were cars and people and more cars.

Drake remembered the robot's comments back in Lab One.

"Well, Rod," he said. "What do you think of uncontrolled environments now?"

"Interesting," Rod replied. "There appears to be a great deal of activity. I am finding that the direct experience of reality can be quite . . . stimulating."

"That it can, son," Weston said.

"Listen," Drake said. "When we get there, how are we going to take Braden down?"

Kenzie turned in the front seat. "My boys will surround the target first," he said. "You people will stay well back until the HRT has the situation under control."

"Agreed," Weston replied. "Just so that we get first crack at Braden once you get him."

Drake knew that Weston was worried about someone else getting to Braden first. Witnesses and prisoners who knew too much had died before, within hours of being captured, often apparent suicides.

Weston wanted no such "suicide" to eliminate the man who would be their key to Diamond.

"Query," Rod said. He was turning in his seat, looking back over his shoulder. "The vehicles approaching from behind are unknown to me. I am familiar with trucks and cars, but these appear to be fundamentally different in design and purpose."

Weston turned, squinting through the rear window. "Motorcycles," he said. "They're a great way to beat the Washington traffic, let me tell you."

Drake was watching the motorcycles now. There were three of them . . . no, four, each carrying two riders, nondescript in leather jackets and colorful helmets. Two were passing the tail security car now, one to the right, one to the left.

Kenzie scowled. "I don't like the looks of this." He reached for the radio handset in the front of the car as the limo crossed onto the Key Bridge. "Shadow Three, this is Shadow One. Watch those . . . Alert! Alert! Bandits on cycles! All units . . ."

The convoy was engulfed in a swirl of movement, but to Drake it felt like slow motion, eerily dreamlike. As though on cue, the two lead motorcycles had accelerated, spurting toward the limo carrying Drake, Weston, and Rod. He could see the riders, each clinging to his driver with one hand, and holding a boxlike Ingram MAC-10 with the other.

The lead car in the convoy came to an abrupt halt, the maneuver so sudden the vehicle skidded until it was almost broadside across the right lane of the bridge. Horns were honking now as other drivers saw danger and reacted, without realizing yet what was happening. In the next instant, Drake's limo slammed into the lead car from behind. The shock wrenched him forward against his seat belt and knocked the radio from Kenzie's hand.

"Son of a bitch!" the FBI agent shouted. He reached down and grabbed his H&K, jacking back the bolt to chamber a round. "Down! Everybody down!"

Gunfire blasted from the two motorcycles in the rear. Drake saw glass explode from the rear limo as it was caught in a vicious crossfire. The tail-car driver wrenched the wheel to the left, apparently trying to sideswipe one of his assailants, but the motorcycle swerved and avoided the clumsy limousine easily. Gunfire from two MAC-10s continued to slam into the car, pocking the doors and hood and splintering the windshield as the high-speed autofire buzzsawed through the passenger compartment.

Kenzie was still screaming for everyone to get down. Drake, however, was not about to let himself be caught inside a stopped car with gunmen firing MAC-10s at him from two sides. In a swift one-two-three of motions, he unfastened his safety belt, yanked the rear-door handle, and slammed his shoulder against the door, catapulting onto the deck of the bridge.

The car door whipping open just in front of him must have startled the right-side motorcyclist because his vehicle swerved sharply, forcing him to put one foot out to brace the machine. The man seated behind him had just been leveling his Ingram at Drake as he rolled onto the street. The sudden swerve dragged his aim up and to the right. The weapon's muzzle flash stabbed, flickering, and Drake heard the unmistakable *snap-snap-snap* of rounds cracking past his head.

The gunman on the left opened fire at the same instant. Drake heard the smash of exploding glass as the rear window shattered. Two more motorcycles, their execution at the tail-end limo complete, raced up from the rear.

Instinctively, Drake groped at his hip for a gun, then remembered that he was unarmed.

The right-hand cyclist recovered control of his machine and closed in, his passenger taking aim. . . .

Within microseconds, Rod had seen the attack and recognized it for what it was. When Kenzie screamed to the passengers to get down, he reached down and snapped the seat belt, not taking the time to unfasten the buckle but simply ripping the tough fabric with his fingers as though it were cotton. He pivoted to the left then, bringing his knees up to his chest, holding the position as the left-hand lead motorcyclist drew even with the car. His hands gripped the seat beneath him, bracing his body.

It was an elementary problem of vectors and forces. At the correct time, his legs unfolded with explosive power, his feet slamming into the door, tearing locking mechanism and hinges with a shriek of tortured metal. Glass filled the air, sparkling.

Like a missile, the limousine's left-rear door hurtled through five feet of empty space and into the approaching motorcycle. Machine and door slammed over onto the street, spilling the riders in a thrashing tangle of limbs.

Rod followed the door, vaulting into the road. He landed in a crouch, spinning to face a second motorcycle as it swerved to miss the cycle that had just been knocked down. The robot reached out, and steel-cored fingers bit into the driver's helmet, puncturing fiberglass like Styrofoam. He yanked, hard, and the motorcyclist's head slammed into the faceplate of his rider, flipping him off the back of the motorcycle, neck broken by the impact.

The driver's head came off in Rod's hand, separating from its body in a scarlet cascade of blood.

On the right side of the car, a third motorcycle with its two riders was bearing down on Drake, who was on his hands and knees. The gunman was already aiming his weapon.

Rod, still turning with the momentum of his first swing, followed through with the movement and let fly, flinging the grisly and now somewhat flattened fiberglass safety helmet in a whipcracking overhand throw. Head and helmet struck the gunman's wrist with the impact of a hard-swung baseball bat, smacking the Ingram away and startling the driver into an uncontrolled skid.

Less than five seconds had passed since the first shots had been fired, less than two since the death of the now headless cyclist. The motorcycle, still bearing his decapitated body, smashed into the lead security car. The Ingram dropped by the rider was still in motion, bouncing along the bridge deck in a series of spinning skips and clatters. Rod's legs pounded as he went into motion, crossing ten meters of space and scooping up the loose weapon in mid-bounce.

The third motorcycle had recovered from its skid and was passing the middle limo now, between the vehicle and the bridge railing. Men were spilling out of the lead security car now, but not to engage in combat. The driver, Rod saw, tumbled out onto the street, the side of his face smashed by a bullet. There was something wrong there, for none of the motorcycle hitmen had fired on the lead car yet.

Filing the data, Rod tracked the right-side motorcycle as it tried to squeeze past the lead car. Rod raised the Ingram in one hand and squeezed the trigger, holding his arm rigid against the sharp, upward recoil. The weapon spat a short burst that slammed into the unarmed rider's back, then jammed, the mechanism fouled by its rough trip across the pavement.

But it was enough. The cycle twisted sideways and struck the safety barrier, slamming the two riders over the barrier and spilling them into space.

It was a good thirty-foot drop to the Potomac, and at least one of the men screamed all the way down.

The fourth and last motorcycle had been holding back. Its driver gunned the engine now and it hurtled up from the rear, the rider crouched low as he leveled his Ingram at Rod. The robot's senses detected the bullets as they snapped past, registering position, velocity, and trajectory by the projectiles' sonic-boom wakes.

There was no time to run or dodge. The motorcycle was trying to thread its way across into the opposite lane of traffic, where terrified drivers were now seeking cover beneath their dashboards, and horns were sounding in a steady, air-raid-siren cacophony that drowned out the shriek of gunfire from the gunman's MAC.

Rod's right arm blurred, the movement too fast for human eyes to follow. The useless MAC-10 in his hand cracked across the intervening space and struck the driver squarely in his chest, crushing sternum and ribs and kicking both men off the back of the motorcycle. The riderless machine slewed sideways and came hurtling toward where Rod was standing.

He sidestepped the unguided missile easily, then whirled as something slammed into his left arm. He had been keeping an automatic tally of the enemies and had thought that all were now accounted for. Two 9mm rounds had just struck him high in the left arm, glancing blows that tore cloth and synthetic plastic skin but left him fully functional. He traced the path of the rounds back. . . .

The FBI agent in the front passenger seat of the lead car was just getting clear of the vehicle, an Uzi in his hands. He'd fired a short burst over the roof of the car at Rod but was now turning toward the middle car where Special Agent Kenzie was scrambling out behind his open car door, still trying to get his hands on his H&K. Drake was just behind Kenzie, still unarmed and very much in the line of fire. The gunman raised his Uzi. . . .

The wreckage of the first motorcycle was a few feet away, still under the car door and wobbling as one of the riders, screaming now in pain, tried to move ruined legs pinned by the machine's weight. Rod reached down and grabbed the motorcycle's front wheel, which was clear of the pavement and still spinning. The shock of hard rubber tore the plastic from his right-hand fingers, but he gripped the wheel and wrenched it free, eliciting another agonized shriek from the injured man under the wreckage. He turned, holding the wheel level, then snapped arm and wrist in unison. Like a huge, black Frisbee, the motorcycle wheel skimmed through the air in a straight path and connected with the traitorous FBI man's head in a gory explosion of blood, bone, and brains. The tire kept flying, wobbling out past the bridge and dropping toward the river. The body with its bloody ruin of a head tottered a moment before dropping the Uzi from limp fingers and crumpling to the pavement.

Rod checked the time on his internal clock. Eight seconds had elapsed from the first shot. Around him, he was aware of the shrieks and screams of wounded gunmen and panicked motorists. Drake and Kenzie were straightening up behind the limo, looking up and down the bridge for other possible threats.

"Good God," a shrill voice called behind Rod. "Who the hell are you, fella, Superman?"

Rod turned and found himself looking down at a slender, mousy-seeming man in glasses and a sport coat. "I am not a man at all," Rod replied. He held up his right hand, where the synthetic skin had been torn away, exposing the black, carbon-lubricated slickness of his titanium-steel alloy fingers. "I should think that would be self-evident."

"Yeah," the man said. His eyes were bugging out from his face as he stared first at Rod's hand, then at his left arm where the workings of miniature hydraulic pistons were exposed, sliding back and forth as the arm flexed. "Yeah, buddy, I can see that!" The man blinked. "What *are* you?"

"A cyborg!" another voice called. "It's incredible!"

"I am a robot," Rod said. "Part of a classified robotics and artificial intelligence program carried out by scientists and engineers of various advanced technology research groups. I have just stopped the attempted assassination of government officials by gunmen in the employ of a drug distribution network."

Rod had been instilled with an understanding of security procedures and knew that RAMROD was classified top secret. No one had ever bothered, however, to teach him how to lie in the event that his cover as an ordinary human was exposed. To Rod's way of thinking there was no use in trying to deny the obvious.

The man was fumbling for a notebook and pen as Rod spoke. Nearby, another man closed in with a Nikormat, the camera's automatic drive going *click-whir-click-whir-click*.

◉ Chapter Ten

THE RICHLY PANELED CONFERENCE ROOM was part of the office suite belonging to the Director of Central Intelligence on the top floor of the CIA's Langley headquarters. Law books and television monitors lined the walls, and the windows on two walls overlooked the lush, northern Virginia countryside.

Admiral Randolph Hewett Cunningham was not watching the scenery. He shoved that morning's *Washington Post* across the conference table with an angry flourish.

CYBERNARC BUSTS DRUG LORD HIT! the paper's headlines proclaimed. The subheader was more explicit: *Intelligent Robot Secret Weapon in Feds' Drug War!* Rod's picture was there beneath the headline, looking human and somewhat remote, almost bored.

"What idiot decided that we were going to let a goddamned *robot* speak to the press!" he thundered.

"It was an accident," Weston replied. "I'll take full responsibility."

In retrospect, it was hard to imagine what he could have done differently. It was plain bad luck that a couple of *Post* reporters and a cameraman had been in one of the other cars on the bridge. In the chaotic aftermath of the firefight, there'd been no way to stop the newsmen from asking their questions, no way to stop Rod from answering in his usual direct way. Weston had descended on the newsmen with threats of legal action against the reporters and their paper if the story was printed, citing national security, but his bluff had been called.

"Damn right you will," the DCI replied. Cunningham, a large man with black horn-rims and white hair, was the newly appointed Director of Central Intelligence.

The third man in the room, with crew-cut salt-and-pepper hair and a permanently combative look on his bulldog features, was Harold Gallagher, the CIA's Executive Director, or EXDIR. He was responsible for the day-to-day internal management of CIA activities. Both EXDIR and the DCI worked with Group Seven and were aware of its projects.

And as the CIA's two senior executives, they had a special and proprietary interest in RAMROD.

"Your robot has become notorious!" Gallagher had never believed in RAMROD and took every opportunity to remind people of the fact. He shook his pen at Weston like an admonishing finger. "Half of Washington is screaming about the 'CIA killer robot' tearing people apart with its bare hands. The other half is laughing itself sick at our two-billion-dollar top-secret motormouth!"

Dr. McDaniels leaned forward at the table, her hands folded in front of her. "Admiral, if I may, this was a totally unforeseen circumstance. Rod fully understands the concept of security. He was simply, at that time, unable to see how it applied to that particular situation."

"What does that mean?"

"It means, sir," Weston said, "that so far as the robot was concerned, it was obvious to anyone just looking at him that he wasn't human, so why pretend that he was? He doesn't . . . understand deception."

"You're telling me that we have a machine that can cheerfully tear people into great bloody chunks without batting an eye, but that it can't tell a *lie*?"

"Rod doesn't know how to suppress or distort the truth, Admiral," McDaniels said.

"You know," Cunningham said. "RAMROD establishes a whole new meaning for the term *smart weapon*. What I don't understand is how it can be so stupid!"

"He's not stupid," McDaniels said. "But the way he thinks is . . . *different.*"

Weston leaned back in his chair, only half listening to McDaniels as she explained the steps that were being taken to prevent a recurrence of yesterday's blunder with the press. The raid intended to pick up Braden had turned into a complete fiasco, and he was wondering what to try next.

As expected, Braden had been warned. Weston had been pretty sure he would be, given Diamond's efficiency in the past. More than ever, he was convinced that the mole had an office somewhere right here in this building.

Weston had ordered the Georgetown raid aborted after the ambush on the bridge. The attack by motorcyclists armed with automatic weapons had obviously been patterned after similar ambushes in Colombia, though this was the first time Weston had heard of it being used in the States. Three of the four FBI HRT men in the rear car had been killed in the crossfire, the fourth seriously wounded. Three agents in the lead car were dead as well, murdered in the opening seconds of the firefight by a gunman who was carrying forged FBI IDs as good as anything ever produced in Langley's printshop. Kenzie and the middle car's driver had escaped without injury, as had Drake and Weston.

There'd been collateral damage as well: nine bystanders wounded—none seriously, fortunately—by stray rounds, flying glass, or bumper-crunching collisions during the eight-second firefight.

It was lucky Rod had been there. Motormouth or not, they all would have been dead without his intervention. Four of the eight cyclists had been killed instantly, and two more had died before reaching Georgetown University Hospital. The two survivors, one of them the driver who'd plunged thirty feet into the Potomac, had been captured and were being held now at FBI headquarters. They'd all been identified as members of the Washington chapter of *Los Salvajes.*

The Savages, once again. It seemed that Diamond had a working relationship with that bunch.

The fake FBI agent, of course, was also dead. As Drake had pointed out to Weston that morning with grim, black humor, the guy had panicked in the fight and lost his head. If he'd stayed down, he might have escaped in the confusion.

The operation blown, Weston had radioed for another car to take them back to their helo at Washington

National immediately, leaving Kenzie to deal with the Georgetown police and the gathering crowd of rubbernecking motorists. Eventually, the police had had to shut down the bridge so that they could remove the bodies, wrecks, and discarded automatic weapons. Later, Kenzie had rounded up another FBI team and raided the Georgetown safe house.

It was empty, of course.

Most disturbing, most frustrating of all, Braden had been found late that same night. The Capital police had fished his body from the tidal basin near the Jefferson Memorial, his hands handcuffed behind his back, his brain punctured by an ice pick inserted through his left ear.

And that left Weston and Group Seven right at the beginning again, with no clues to Diamond or his whereabouts.

"Cybernarc!" The EXDIR snorted, looking at the newspaper headline again. "What the hell kind of name is *Cybernarc*? Was this your cyborg's idea? Or yours?"

"Actually, that was our newspaper friends," Weston said.

"And inaccurate," McDaniels said stiffly. "Rod is *not* a cyborg."

EXDIR scowled. "What's the difference?"

"Cybernetics is any system having to do with functions of control or coordination," McDaniels said in her best lecture-hall tone. "By that definition, the timers for a city's traffic lights or the CPU in a computer are 'cybernetic.' *Cyborg* comes from 'cybernetic organism,' a mixture of man and machine. A man in an iron lung would qualify. Rod is a robot, an android robot if you like, a machine designed to look and act like a human. I'd like to know when the news reporters are going to start getting their facts straight when they deal with scientific matters."

"Actually, sir," Weston said, "the story's inaccuracies may work to our advantage."

"How do you figure that?" Admiral Cunningham asked.

"We can use them. 'Cybernarc.' It's kind of flashy. And it's misleading. Hell, 'narc' is street slang for a narcotics agent. No self-respecting Federal agent would ever call *himself* a narc." He slapped the newspaper on the tabletop with the back of his hand. "This is garbage, Admiral. Half-truths and distortions. We can deny what we want and be believed, simply because this is all so damned unbelievable in the first place."

"You can say that again," Gallagher said.

"And not only that, but we can put out a few distortions of our own. Like that we have an army of these things out tracking down dope pushers, dealers, corrupt city officials. It'll make the bad guys nervous, if only because they'll be wondering what we're really up to. And nervous people make mistakes."

Admiral Cunningham pushed back in his executive's chair, fingers drumming. He pursed his lips. "I like it," he said at last. "Especially the disinformation angle. I'll speak to Ed about it." He leaned forward and made a note on a legal pad in front of him. Edward Hernshaw was the CIA's Public Affairs Officer.

"Is that going to be enough, Admiral?" Gallagher

asked. "This damned robot silliness could blow up in our faces."

"My guess is that the papers will drop the story completely in a day or two. It reads like silly season stuff." He looked hard at Weston. "I don't want you to think this has you off the hook," he added. "But we'll see how the headlines run for the next few days."

"Yes, sir."

"Right," Cunningham said. "Where is the robot now?"

"At the Farm," McDaniels said. "We took him back last night. He suffered minor external damage in the gun battle—nothing serious. They're patching him up."

"And how would you evaluate his first, ah, field test?"

"From what I've heard," McDaniels replied, "he handled himself well. Certainly he came up with some ingenious expedients. I'd say he passed with flying colors."

"More like flying car doors, MAC-10s, and motorcycle tires," Weston added. "Not to mention a flying head. I checked. He got off exactly three rounds with a captured Ingram before the thing jammed. Everything else he improvised on the spot. As a raw, two-fisted-death combat machine, he is incredible!"

"If you can teach him to watch his mouth, then, we might have something." Cunningham folded his hands for a moment, seeming to study them. "It's still your opinion that RAMROD could be applied to Group Seven's special projects?"

"After seeing him in action yesterday? More than ever."

"Doctor? What do you think?"

She did not answer immediately.

"You have reservations?"

She hesitated before replying. "If Rod has any weaknesses, they're in his ability to work with people. To *understand* people. He still has trouble with slang and ambiguous language. Metaphors throw him. So does humor. He tends to look for the literal meaning of words."

"This . . . gaff of his on the bridge yesterday," Cunningham said. "It still worries me."

"Rod's big advantage is that he learns very, *very* fast. He will never repeat a mistake. But because he *is* intelligent in every sense of the word, he *will* make mistakes . . . like any thinking being."

"Isn't that a contradiction? He makes mistakes *because* he's intelligent?"

"Intelligence means being free to make mistakes, Admiral. He doesn't just blindly follow rote programming. And because Rod's not human, his mistakes won't be human ones. He may act in ways that we would find . . . bizarre. Certainly unpredictable."

"All the more reason to scrap the idea of using the robot in any covert op," Gallagher said. "It's too dangerous. God . . . what if the thing had run wild on the bridge yesterday, killing innocent bystanders?"

"He wouldn't *do* that," McDaniels insisted.

Cunningham looked at Weston. "Have you considered this in your planning, James? It would be a shame to end a two-billion-dollar program because a damned

intelligent piece of covert hardware wasn't . . . predict-
able."

"Like she says, Admiral. Rod learns fast."

"That may not be enough." Cunningham looked at
McDaniels. "Let me ask you this, Doctor. You say the
robot thinks for itself. Could you program it so that it
had to obey the orders given to it? Some sort of fail
safe, a backup, just in case."

Her lips compressed. "It would be possible," she
said after a moment. "I don't believe it's necessary."

"The plan was to team RAMROD with a human op-
erative, correct?"

Weston nodded. "We thought that would minimize
the risks. We've used several subjects in the PARET
training so far. One of them is a combat veteran, a Navy
SEAL who works quite well with Rod."

"Lieutenant Drake."

"That's right."

"I've read the reports. He went through a pretty
rough time. How is he handling it?"

"He's recovering. And he has a serious . . . commit-
ment to tracking these people down."

"Can you trust him?"

Weston thought about the question. How well Drake
was coping with what had happened was something
only Drake himself could know. He seemed to be handling it, but Weston knew that people did not simply
walk away from that sort of shock.

"Yes, sir," Weston said. "I think I can."

"You'd better be sure," Cunningham said. He
glanced at McDaniels. "See what you can work up for
a fail safe. Some way for your boy to pull the robot's

plug if things go wrong." He shook his head. "Trust is becoming an increasingly valuable commodity around here."

Diamond was very much on everyone's mind. The mole had been busy lately, organizing the SNOWDROP ambush and covering Braden's trail, tracking down Drake and organizing that attempted assassination, setting up the hit on the bridge in Georgetown. The downgraded assessment on Drake's report was probably Diamond's handiwork, as were the forged credentials on the bogus FBI man and the death of Braden hours after the CIA contract pilot had been identified as a suspect.

Diamond had to be found, and quickly. God knew how much more damage he could do before he was run to ground.

Since the CIA was in charge of RAMROD, the op tagged AMBER HARVEST had to be reviewed by Agency executives. Its importance was evidenced by the ranks of the people in attendance.

Drake was there as RAMROD's military expert, feeling distinctly uncomfortable in a vaultlike security room full of suits. Some of the executive types at the table he knew: Weston, of course, and he knew Admiral Cunningham by reputation. Harold T. Gallagher, the EXDIR, was present, going over notes he'd made at an earlier meeting with Weston and the DCI. Drake had met EXDIR during the *Achille Lauro* incident, when Gallagher had been the CIA's chief logistics officer and responsible for arranging the airfields, planes, boats, or rendezvous sites for covert SEAL and Delta ops on

Agency business. Later, he'd been promoted to Deputy
Director of Administration (DDA), and when Admiral
Cunningham had been appointed DCI, he'd been
picked as the Agency's Executive Director.

Drake also knew Dr. Theodore Godiesky, the CIA
S&T man who was now working at RAMROD, and General Maxwell Sinclair, the U.S. Joint Special Operations
Command liaison with the CIA and the only man in the
room besides himself in uniform.

The rest of the men were strangers to Drake. Dr. Vin-
cent Weis, from the Office of Imagery Analysis. Greg
Sandervall, the Deputy Director of Intelligence (DDI).
Peter Babcock, the assistant DDA. Taylor Smolleck,
from the Office of Logistics. And there was the spy-
master himself, Walton Crawford, Deputy Director of
Operations, or DDO. It was Crawford who was in
charge of the clandestine aspects of CIA activity, including covert operations in other countries, and Drake
understood that he was running the Agency's narcotics
division.

The buzz of conversation among the men in the room
stilled as Cunningham stood at the head of the table.
"If we can begin, gentlemen," the DCI said. "Okay.
As all of you know, we have a situation here. That situation calls himself Diamond. The purpose of this meeting is to brainstorm ways to flush our friend Diamond
into the open."

The silence became, if possible, even more intense.
Drake knew what each of them was thinking. There was
a real possibility that one of the men in that room—or
one of these men's subordinates—was Diamond. By

openly discussing the problem, Cunningham was daring Diamond to eavesdrop.

Which, of course, was the idea. Only Weston, Drake, and the DCI were aware of that aspect of the plan.

"First off," Cunningham said, consulting his notes, "we have an ID on the bogus FBI agent. He's been identified as Charles Wilson Vanecki. For the past twelve years he's been a CIA employee, Office of Security."

There was a low murmur around the table at the news. "What's the chance that he was Diamond?" EXDIR asked.

Cunningham looked thoughtful. "It's a possibility, but not a good one. If Diamond is the mastermind everyone thinks he is, he wouldn't have risked himself in the bridge ambush. But OS does think that Vanecki might have been Diamond's pipeline into the Company."

"You mean Diamond might not be part of the Agency after all?" Godiesky asked. "He just had access to Agency records through this Vanecki?"

"A distinct possibility," Cunningham replied. "For the time being, we are working on that assumption."

Drake could almost sense the relaxation in the atmosphere around the table. Perhaps the Agency didn't have a mole after all. That meant there would be no fingers pointing at the department head who had hired a *traitor*. . . .

"What about this Delgado?" Pete Babcock asked.

"Yes, Delgado," Cunningham said. He nodded at Weston. "We have RAMROD to thank for that lead. Delgado has been positively implicated in this case, a high-ranking DAS man who is suspected of working for the Salazar drug cartel as well."

"Shit," EXDIR said. "He was going to be our inside man in the DAS. We should find him. He could tell us how badly our intelligence operations down there have been penetrated."

"Can we locate him?" Sandervall wanted to know. "Have the FBI pick him up for questioning?"

"Unfortunately," Cunningham replied, "Delgado is no longer in the country."

"How did that happen?" Gallagher demanded. "I thought he was on our watch list, along with Braden! Damn it, he's our only other link to Diamond!"

"It looks like he knew that. A man matching Delgado's description boarded a Viasa flight at Dulles last night, bound for Bogotá." Cunningham gestured toward the Imagery Analysis man. "Doctor?"

Dr. Weis opened the briefcase in front of him, removed a manila folder, and extracted several photographs. He passed these around the table.

"We got these in this morning from NPIC," Weis said. He pronounced the acronym of the National Photographic Interpretation Center "en-pick."

When one of the photos came to him, Drake held it by its edges and examined it closely. Looking down into a courtyard as though shot from a second-story window, it had the characteristic negative-image quality of an infrared photo. An automobile, a Mercedes, was parked in front of a building, its front end glowing with the engine's heat. Twelve men stood about the courtyard in various poses, caught in mid-motion: sentries carrying assault rifles, the car's driver standing by the door, two men nearby shaking hands. An arrow pointed to one of them.

Drake felt a chill. Despite the distortions of thermal imaging, he recognized the mustache, the lean features.

Delgado. The man he'd known as Esposito.

"Satellite photos, Doctor?" Taylor Smolleck wanted to know.

"Taken from an altitude of 126 miles by a KH-12 at 0230 hours this morning. This is an enlargement of the courtyard in front of the Salazar family hacienda on the Gulf Coast. The arrow points to the man we believe is Delgado."

"The evidence indicates that Delgado bugged out as soon as he heard about the Key Bridge ambush," Cunningham said. "Our satellite reconnaissance suggests that the private army guarding *La Fortaleza Salazar* has stepped up its defenses in the last twelve hours, doubled its guard, put extra patrols into the jungle. . . . In short, gentlemen, Delgado has jumped into a hole, and now the Salazars are slamming the lid."

"Why?" Gallagher asked. The EXDIR looked up from one of the photos. "Is he afraid we're going to grab him? Make him tell us who Diamond is?"

Crawford laughed. "More likely he's afraid of Diamond!" the DDO said. "Probably he figures Diamond wants to get him before we can. He might know about what happened to Braden. That'd be enough to make our Colombian friend very nervous!"

"That is my assessment as well," Cunningham said. He looked at the men around the table once more, as though measuring them. "Gentlemen, we are opening a new operations file, code-named AMBER HARVEST. This will be a covert operation aimed at securing the person of Luis Delgado-Valasquez." He waited out the sudden stir and murmur of voices. "I am aware of the risk that Diamond will learn of our plans, but I believe it is a worthwhile risk . . . and one we must take. The operation will be organized in such a way that Diamond will not be able to sabotage the mission without giving himself away. And if we get Delgado, I am convinced we will get Diamond as well." He cracked a smile. "So if one of you is Diamond, you might as well give up now!"

A ripple of nervous laughter circled the table.

"No takers? Then perhaps we can assume that Diamond is elsewhere. Now, the operation will be run by a JSOC team under the direction of General Sinclair. Included in the team will be an operational unit of Project RAMROD."

"RAMROD?" Gallagher snapped. "Why bring *that* into it?"

"Because AMBER HARVEST provides us with an ideal opportunity for field-testing RAMROD. This is part of our agreement with Group Seven, Harry, as you will recall." Cunningham gestured toward Drake. "Lieutenant Drake here, who has considerable experience with the system, will be in charge."

"How do you feel having a robot in your squad?" General Sinclair asked. The others laughed.

"No problem, General," Drake replied.

In truth, he wasn't sure how he felt. He'd seen Rod in action and he'd been impressed, damned impressed. But suppose the robot pulled another goof . . . the jungle equivalent of talking to reporters? The mission could be aborted . . . or worse.

But despite Cunningham's suggestion that Vanecki had been the CIA mole, the chances were still pretty good that one of the men at the table was Diamond. The plan worked out with Weston and the DCI hours earlier counted on Diamond learning about AMBER HARVEST and adding a few twists of his own.

Twists that would implicate the traitor within the CIA's ranks.

It also depended on Rod functioning flawlessly and intelligently in a true uncontrolled environment. Was Rod ready for that kind of test?

He didn't know.

Later, Weston caught up to Drake in a corridor. "Lieutenant? How are you doing? Really?"

Drake's eyebrows rose. "Fine, sir. No problem."

"You don't have to do this, you know."

"I did ask to go."

"I know. But some of us . . . well, we're wondering how you're handling what happened. Your family."

Drake kept his emotions clamped down, hard. "I would be lying, Mr. Weston, if I said it doesn't bother me. But it's under control. Believe me."

"You've never entirely believed in RAMROD. As a combat-operational system. If that's a problem . . ."

Drake sighed. "Mr. Weston, at this point, if you ordered me to stay behind, I'd swim to Colombia. I *want* these people. And I'll do it with or without a robot as a sidekick."

"That's not exactly a reassuring answer, son," Weston said. "The mission is to capture Delgado. Not to . . . to avenge your wife and kid."

Drake's eyes locked with Weston's. Neither man

spoke for several seconds. "Yes, sir. That is understood. Will there be anything else?"

"No. Just . . . good luck."

Drake turned and walked away, his emotions still rigidly in check.

◉ *Chapter Eleven*

THE NUCLEAR SUBMARINE *John Marshall* was an old Ethan Allen–class boat. Originally commissioned as a Polaris boomer in 1962, she'd been converted to an attack sub in 1981, then reconverted in the mid-eighties for the transport role. *Marshall*'s missile tubes had been removed to make room for up to sixty-five troops and their equipment, and fittings on her afterdeck were designed to accommodate Dry Deck Shelters that held a pair of Navy swimmer delivery vehicles.

The *Marshall* had been slated for retirement in 1990, but cuts in the Navy's budget for such luxuries as special-mission, frogman-carrying submarines had forced her indefinite retention. *Marshall* had slipped her moorings at Little Creek four days before and, traveling underwater at a steady twenty knots, was now approaching the north Colombian coast. On board were Lieutenant Drake and Rod, together with two four-man SEAL elements, the strike force for AMBER HARVEST.

Drake had been watching Rod with increasing misgivings during the voyage south through the Bahamas and the Windward Passage. He watched the robot now

152

as he applied talcum powder to the inside of his own jet-black wet suit, preparing for the mission.

Rod needed no wet suit. Normally, while wearing what RAMROD personnel referred to as his Civilian Mod, Rod looked about as ordinary as it was possible to look—a tall man with light brown hair and pleasant features, somewhat on the rangy side, and with the somewhat disconcerting habit of turning his head while he spoke with you, as though he were watching the room rather than any one person in it.

He had arrived on board the *Marshall* in full Combat Mod, however, and looked anything but normal.

Blue-black, low-gloss titanium-steel in the place of synthetic skin seemed to drink the direct overhead lighting of the troop compartment. Legs, arms, and the massive, armored plastron over chest and back appeared bulky, giving Rod the hulking silhouette of a football linebacker.

Yet for all his bulk and mass, Rod moved as lithely and as easily in Combat Mod as he did when he looked human. The openings at his joints exposed the intricacies of overlapping armor plate, of wires and miniature hydraulic pistons that worked together under microcomputer direction to deliver tremendous power to each of his movements. Though powerful, the robot had the grace of a cat . . . although the way he turned and held his head from time to time still had a mechanical quality, and the sheer precision of his movements was eerily inhuman. His hands were no larger than normal—they could not be if he was expected to use weapons or controls designed for human beings—but they had the same lusterless, light-drinking matte finish as the rest of his body, and a touch proved that they were made of the same unyielding titanium-steel alloy.

When he was wearing Combat Mod, only Rod's head and facial features appeared unchanged, and the bulk of his new body made his head seem curiously small and out of place, recessed in the well between his shoulders that received his armored neck. It looked, in fact, as though he were wearing some sort of bulky space suit. In combat, Rod would also wear a special helmet to protect the vulnerable and unarmored head and its extremely sensitive, broad-spectrum optical gear.

That helmet gave Rod a decidedly alien look. Those cool, gray eyes were masked behind a black visor strip that fed visual, thermal, and radar imagery directly to his visual processors, bypassing the eyes entirely.

A power cable trailed across the deck as the robot topped off his batteries.

"Lord Almighty," one of the SEALs in the compartment said, watching Rod as the machine made some minute adjustment to the battle helmet in its lap. Boatswain Chief Randy Campano shook his head in admiration. "That sucker is damn near invisible sittin' in here with the lights on. He's gonna disappear in that jungle."

"They say you've worked with ol' Bot before, Lieutenant," RN/3 Matt Zitterman said. "Think he'll hold up in a stand-up fight?"

Drake shrugged. "All I can say is he's managed okay so far."

"Stow it, Zit. Don't you worry about ol' Rambot," GM/1 Carl Hoskins said. "You saw him on the gunnery range, didn't you? Hell, he can outshoot any man in this compartment! You just worry about your own proficiency scores!"

"Aw, up yours, Hoss," MT/2 Joshua Gordon said in his soft, west Texas drawl. "You know as well as the rest of us that it's not the shootin' that counts in a firefight. It's what you're *made* of."

"Well, hell's bells, Rod oughta do okay then," Zitterman observed. "Looks to me like a LAW rocket wouldn't more'n scratch him!"

Drake shook his head as he listened to the banter. They'd spent the last four days living together underwater, but Rod had spoken little, volunteered nothing. As H-hour approached he could sense the SEALs' growing curiosity about their strange comrade, and he knew that all of them were wondering the same thing: could they count on Rod in combat?

The hell of it was, Drake himself wasn't sure how he would answer. Rod's silence seemed like brooding, though Drake knew it was silly to attribute such a human state of mind to a machine. Drake began peeling on his wet suit, turning the question over in his mind. How *would* Rod behave in combat?

There was no question of Rod's combat ability, but the one time he'd been under fire for real, the robot had taken down the bad guys on his own. He'd not worked with human soldiers as part of a team.

Oh, Drake and Rod had trained briefly together with the eight SEALs at Dam Neck, but only in the mechanics of egressing from the sub and making their way ashore. There'd been no time for more than that and a couple of turns at the firing range. The SEALs seemed to accept him, had nicknamed him "Bot" and "Rambot," but when it came to working with him in a combat environment, none of them, Drake included, knew exactly what to expect.

If Rod had been a human member of a combat team, that would have been a sure recipe for suicide. In a firefight there was one absolute: each member of the team had to be able to depend on every other member.

The robot was an unknown quantity, however. Recognizing that there simply was not enough time to train the covert operations team to accept and use Rod as they would a human comrade, Weston, General Sinclair, and the mission planners had elected to incorporate him as just another piece of equipment. In their briefings to the SEALs before embarkation, they had stressed the fact that Rod was a machine, as much a tool as the weapons they carried.

That was why Weston had ordered Rod not to speak to the other SEALs except in direct response to their questions. It was felt that if the men began talking freely with Rod, they would quickly begin thinking of him as a person. So far, no one had ventured a guess as to whether that would be good or bad. It was safer, though, to think of him as a *thing* of unknown potential, rather than as a man who might let them down at a crucial point with some distinctly unmanlike goof.

Drake could already tell that Langley's strategy was not working, however. Rod still *looked* like a man—however strange he might appear in Combat Mod—and when he spoke, it was with the same low, precise, and very human-sounding speech that Rod used at the Farm. It was impossible for the eight other SEALs to live with Rod for four days, to speak with him and listen to his replies, and not think of him as a man.

The enlisted SEALs had paired off, each man applying stick camouflage to the portions of his partner's face exposed by his wet-suit hood when there was a metallic bang and the forward watertight door swung open. Captain Wyler stepped across the raised kneeknocker and into the compartment. Zitterman called attention on deck, and the other SEALs straightened up. Rod, interestingly enough, remained seated. The robot had not received PARET training in military courtesy.

The submarine's skipper only glanced at the robot, then turned and addressed the SEALs, hands on hips. "At ease," he said. "Okay, gentlemen. We're twelve miles off the coast, at a depth of sixty-three feet. We took a periscope sighting on your objective, and your compass bearing will be one-eight-seven. Sunset was four hours ago and it's a dark night. Looks like a perfect evening for a swim." He paused, looking at each of the nine, black-faced SEALs in turn. "I just wanted to repeat the word I had from Washington. After the SDVs drop you froggies off, they're to beat it back to the *Marshall.* As soon as they're stowed, my orders are to RTB. Once you boys hit the beach, there's no coming back."

"Understood, Captain," Drake said. "We have . . . other arrangements for pickup."

"Well, you damned well better. It's a hell of a long swim back to Norfolk!" Captain Wyler glanced again at Rod, still sitting in the corner. "You have all the gear you need." It was a statement, not a question.

"That's affirmative, sir."

"Well, if you're ready, the sooner I have you off my boat, the sooner I can take my merry crew back to civilization, women, and beer. And the sooner you can get on with . . . whatever the hell you're supposed to be doing out here."

"Yes, sir," Drake replied. Captain Wyler had not been briefed on the SEALs part of the op. As much as possible, each segment of the mission was isolated from the rest, the individual players knowing nothing but their own part in the drama. He smiled. "And if anyone asks, Captain, you never saw us."

"Take care, then." The Captain grinned. "Don't start any wars that you guys can't finish yourselves!"

"Aye aye, Captain." Hoskins said, chuckling. "We always finish what we start!"

We finish what we start. Drake thought about that as he buckled his weight belt, then checked wrist compass, depth gauge, and watch. He had some business to settle with Señor Luis Delgado.

Business that the Colombian had started, but that Drake was going to finish.

For a moment, the memories of blood, gunfire, and horror threatened to close in on him again. He pushed them aside, concentrating on his responsibilities as dive master. Grimly, he went to each of the other SEALs in the compartment, checking their equipment, harnesses, and weapons. Each man was fully rigged out in black wet suit, fins, mask and snorkel, and Mark VI semiclosed circuit SCUBA. Each man carried a sealed equipment bag holding his boots, ammo, canteens, medical kits, and other dry gear the team would need ashore. As their *SE*a, *A*ir, and *L*and acronym suggested,

SEALs took pride in operating effectively both in and out of the water.

When he was certain that every man's equipment was functioning and complete, and after Chief Campano had checked him, Drake gave the order for the team to begin cycling through *Marshall*'s escape trunk. Rod completed some last-minute adjustments on his helmet and put it on. Armored, with angled surfaces and no recognizable features except for the optical visor strip, the helmet gave Rod a sinister, malevolent look.

They locked out of the chamber two at a time, swimming through the hatch opening as soon as the airlock was flooded and into the inky blackness of the sea. Drake went through with Rod, who moved with extra caution. Where the divers had their weight belts and equipment adjusted to give them neutral buoyancy, Rod in his massive Combat Mod armor would sink like a stone if he stepped off the submarine's deck. As they'd practiced at Little Creek days before, Rod attached himself to the sub's deck with a safety line, standing clear as the swimmers, working in the shifting, murky light of handheld lanterns, began unshipping the SDVs from the Dry Deck Shelters.

The Swimmer Delivery Vehicle (SDV) EX-VIII was a minisub capable of ferrying six men and their equipment for long distances underwater. Designed for covert insertions, it was termed a "wet" submarine because the crew, passenger, and cargo compartments were fully flooded during underwater operations. For this mission, two SDVs would be used, each carrying five passengers plus an operator who would return the minisub to the *Marshall* after the swimmers were dropped off at the beach.

Drake took his place aboard the lead SDV next to Rod, turned off his SCUBA, and connected himself to the vehicle's on-board life support. Moments later, there was a gentle whirr as the sub's electric battery motor began propelling the vehicle swiftly through the black water.

In the dim glow from a chemical light in the compartment, Drake looked again at Rod. The effect was startling. With its helmet on, the robot definitely looked far more like a machine, worse, like some armored alien monster in a science fiction epic, than a man.

He wondered what Rod was thinking.

Rod had an easier time on land than underwater. There were plans on the drawing board, he knew, for units that would give him superb undersea mobility, but those would not be ready for some time yet. For now, once he left the SDV, he was limited to moving clumsily along the bottom like an old-time, hard-hat salvage diver. It was with something closely akin to relief that he raised his armored head above the water and scanned the beach, now only a few meters ahead.

The night-vision light-intensifier electronics of his combat helmet were working perfectly. Under LI, the strip of beach seemed as distinct and as brightly lit to the robot as it would have appeared to a human at high noon. As he carefully swept the landing area, readouts overlaid the image relayed to his visual processing centers, giving range, bearing, and a set of targeting crosshairs.

Momentarily, he switched to infrared, and a thermal view replaced the LI image. Water and sky turned black, while cliff face and sand showed in mingled shades of gray and green. Two hot spots fifty meters to the left marked SM/3 Ben Saylor and TM/3 Nathan Isaacson, the two SEALs charged with going ashore first to check out the beach. Under IR imaging, Rod could see them crouched among the sea-wet rocks. Twin trails of yellow-warm patches leading up from the water's edge showed where they'd crossed the beach.

Except for them, the bridge was deserted. Isaacson was flashing a hooded penlight toward the sea, signaling the other SEALs to come ashore.

It would have made more sense to send Rod ahead as the point, of course. His senses were far sharper than those of men, even when they carried LI scopes and thermal viewers. Rod accepted with his usual equanimity the decision to stick with standard procedure in this case. Rod was aware that his human comrades still had a lot to learn about his capabilities.

They were, after all, only human.

Like the sea monster of a late-night movie, Rod rose dripping from the surf. Ahead, the cliff rose thirty feet above the beach, a tumble of fallen boulders and sheer rock. Tilting his head back, the movement somewhat clumsy under the added weight of the armored helmet, he scanned the cliff top. The seaward wall of the Salazar hacienda was just visible a kilometer to the east.

There were no sentries in sight.

The other SEALs emerged from the sea at Rod's back, but he was aware of their movements, of the slight break in the ocean's rhythms, and of the sucking, liquid sounds of their bare feet on wet sand. Leaving deep prints, Rod moved toward the boulder spill where Isaacson and Saylor were crouching.

"Yo, Rambot!" Saylor whispered. "Snap it up!"

Rod did not comment as he unhooked his harness and lowered the equipment load to the sand. The soft *slap-slap-slap* of running feet carried above the rumble and hiss of the surf, and the other SEALs dropped to their bellies in the darkness around them, facing out, weapons at the ready.

As was usual on this type of mission, the weapons represented the personal choice of individual SEALs. Saylor, Carter, and Isaacson carried H&K MP5SD3s with their heavy, distinctive sound-suppressor barrels. Drake's weapon of choice was an Uzi SMG. Gordon, Hoskins, and Zitterman all carried M-16s, while Chief Campano preferred the ruggedness and drop-it-in-the-mud reliability of a Soviet-made AK-47. TM/2 Jake Yancey, the sniper of the group, was already unpacking the case that held his broken-down Model 500 Long Range Weapon, a monster sniper's rifle that fired a .50 caliber Browning cartridge and was accurate at ranges of over a kilometer.

All of the SEALs carried the SEAL-special Mark 22 Model O 9mm Hush Puppies. The holsters on their hips had been modified to accommodate the pistols complete with their outsized sound suppressors.

Like Drake, Rod carried an Uzi. Drake's preference for the Israeli-made SMG seemed to have carried through to the robot in the PARET training sessions back at the Farm.

Quickly, silently, they broke out the rest of their

equipment. Their tanks, fins, and masks went into a cache among the boulders, to be picked up later by another team or abandoned, depending on the situation. From their sealed gear bags they produced heavy boots fit for climbing, meter upon meter of rope, boonie hats and camo jackets, and combat harnesses with full ammo pouches.

Saylor and Isaacson, serving as guides, would wear BM 8208 light-intensifier goggles for the hike to the objective. The rest of the men would rely on their own eyes, since the one-kilo goggles sharply restricted the wearer's field of view, a serious liability in this sort of operation. Each SEAL wore a radio headset with a voice-activated lip mike and an earplug speaker. Though range was limited to a few kilometers, the radios would provide tactical communications for the entire team.

RN/3 Wyatt Carter, meanwhile, assembled the team's backpack radio and broadcast their first message. "Snowdance. Snowdance. Snowdance," he called, whispering into the mike.

Seconds later, the response came through his headset, loud enough for Rod's sensitive hearing to pick up the words. At the same time, he heard the words through his own internal radio circuits. "Blue Ranger . . . Warpath. Warpath. Warpath."

"Mission is go," Carter told the others.

Drake was studying the top of the cliff. "Let's do it."

The climb was an easy one. Ten minutes later, the team was crouching among the coconut palms at the top, one hundred meters from the west wall of the hacienda. The coast road ran through the jungle to their right, and beyond was the night-black bulk of the jungle-carpeted mountains. On their left, the cliff dropped to the sea, ten meters below.

Rod studied the objective. There were lights on, but the walls were not lit, and most of the interior grounds were dark. With thermal imaging, he could see several sentries patrolling inside the wall in military-looking camo fatigues, carrying automatic weapons.

"Right," Drake said. "Let's make for the hide."

The plan called for using SNOWDROP's OP site as a staging point for the raid. Silently, the SEALs began moving through the trees, the hulking black robot bringing up the rear.

The security guard adjusted a knob on the television monitor, brightening the image. The IR camera was working perfectly, turning the night beyond the hacienda perimeter into day. Nine man-sized shapes were moving through the trees one hundred meters to the east. A tenth shape, larger, a bit fuzzier than the others, was with them. The guard tried to resolve the picture, then gave up. Probably the tenth man's uniform was heavy enough to block his body heat, fuzzing his image on the scanner.

He picked up a telephone and stabbed the intercom button. "*Alo . . . Jefe?*" he said. He listened a moment, then identified himself. "This is Security. They are here. *Sí, sí . . .* in the jungle. I see nine or ten of them, no more. You'd better tell Luis and Don Roberto."

It was happening exactly as his bosses had told him it would.

● Chapter Twelve

THEY LEFT THREE MEN at the hillside OP above the hacienda: Carter with the radio, Yancey with the .50 caliber sniper's rifle, and Chief Campano as spotter and command backup. The rest of the team, six men plus Rod, moved down the slope toward the front entrance to *La Fortaleza Salazar*. Their plan was simple and direct. They would enter the Salazar compound by going over the wall, neutralizing any sentries they came across, then find and force someone to tell them where within the compound Delgado was staying. After that, they would find, grab, and drug their target, then sneak out the way they'd come with their prisoner unconscious and slung across Rod's broad, armored back.

The mission, Drake thought as the team sprinted across the coast road at a spot where trees blocked the view from the hacienda walls, would have been impossible without the robot. The SEALs were depending on his superior senses to alert them to danger, and on his strength to haul their prisoner away afterward without slowing them down.

He dropped into a drainage ditch at the far side of

the road, then checked the area. There was still no sign that the enemy had spotted them.

Drake looked at Rod. The robot was scanning with eerie, mechanically precise movements of his helmet, the Uzi SMG clutched in one hand as casually as a pistol.

"Anything?" Drake whispered.

"No."

Drake gestured toward the compound wall. "Check it out."

The robot was gone, moving so silently that he scarcely seemed to disturb the thick vegetation.

As he crouched in the darkness with the other SEALs Drake decided that it would do no good to wonder about whether the robot was going to screw up on this mission. Whatever mistakes he might make, the team would have to deal with them exactly as if he'd been a human soldier.

Cybernarc.

He was the unknown component of the mission now.

The range to the compound wall was eighty meters. The trees and vegetation had been cleared to create a killing zone extending for half that distance from the hacienda wall, but Rod crossed the open ground without incident. Reaching the base of the wall near the southwest corner, he crouched in the shadows for a moment, listening as no human possibly could.

The loudest sounds were those of the jungle at night, the high-pitched, continuous peeping and chirping of tree frogs, crickets, and other nocturnal fauna. One by one, Rod recorded the sounds, analyzed them, then let his computer aural processors filter them out. From his point of view—or in this case, listening—the chirping sounds vanished.

The sounds of wind and surf were next, white noise easily filtered.

What was left was a silence almost absolute. Increasing his aural sensitivity, Rod could hear the faintest of stirrings among the ferns eighty meters behind him, the scratch of fabric on skin as one of the SEALs shifted his position slightly in the ditch. Blanking out those sounds, he kept listening, trying to catch traces of movement inside the hacienda wall.

There . . . another scratch of cloth on skin. And another sound, the slow *swish-swish-swish* of fatigues interspersed with the tread of rubber-soled boots on hard earth. The *chink* of metal. A man was walking on the other side of the wall.

More sounds . . . the clink and jingle of a chain, the snuffling sounds of an animal, more footsteps. A dog on a leash, accompanied by a sentry on his rounds. Rod plotted the sounds, points of light appearing on a window map overlaying his visual field. The map, generated from spy-satellite shots taken only a few days ago, showed the sprawling, U-shaped hacienda, several outlying buildings including a garage and a stable, and the swimming pool and hedge-barricaded patio off the southeast corner of the house. The only sounds of movement he could detect within the wall came from the guards just on the other side of the wall. Others were probably on the grounds, but too distant for him to pick up.

Still scanning, he blanked out the human sounds and

listened further, checking for the low-frequency hum of an electron flow. Nothing . . . nothing close by, at least. The objective was not guarded by an electronic alarm system, then.

He opened his radio communications line, adjusting the frequency to correspond with one of the two available channels used by the SEAL personal comm sets.

Blue Ranger, RAMROD. A watcher would not have realized he was communicating at all, for there was no sound. Since Rod's vocalizations were produced by a digital vodor, there was no reason why the words had to be converted first to sound, then reconverted to radio waves. Rod simply manufactured the radio waves directly.

RAMROD, Blue Ranger. Drake's words sounded internally in the same way, for the same reasons, a kind of electronic telepathy. *Go ahead.*

Aural scans indicate two sentries, one with a dog, positioned within fifteen meters of my position. He had to make the report fast and succinct. Someone in the compound might be listening in with a channel scanner. *No electronic alarms. No sonic alarms.*

Rog. We're moving up.

Rod readjusted his audio levels and waited. Moments later, the SEALS moved in out of the darkness, leapfrogging ahead two at a time.

The fortress remained quiet . . . and apparently unsuspecting.

The SEAL team waited until Rod signaled that the two sentries on the other side of the wall were far enough away that they wouldn't hear the metallic clanks of thrown grapnels over the *peep-peep-peeping* of nocturnal jungle wildlife. The wall was made of stucco-plastered concrete blocks stacked ten feet high, topped by coils of razor wire and shards of broken glass set in concrete.

Drake watched as Gordon and Zitterman stepped back and gently tossed grappling hooks up and over the wall. Both caught. Weapons slung, Isaacson and Saylor started walking up the wall as their companions braced the climbing ropes at the bottom. Each man carried a canvas sheet that he laid across the razor wire at the top, and extra lengths of rope that he lowered down the far side and secured in place. With no more sound than the metallic rustle of the wire as they rolled across the top, five SEALs slipped over the wall and dropped into the compound at the far side.

Drake and Rod went next, the robot lifting its 420-plus pounds effortlessly up the line hand over hand. Drake, moving more slowly, paused to snap off several jagged shards of glass beneath the canvas padding at the top, then used one of the descent lines to drop to the neatly manicured lawn on the other side.

There were lights on near the pool and in the house. The SEALs crouched among the shadows. There was a sharp, flat thump in the night, then another. Saylor materialized out of the darkness a moment later, a Hush Puppy in his hand, signaling quietly. One sentry and the dog had been taken out. The other sentry was still on the hoof, somewhere off to the northwest.

Using hand signs, Drake deployed the team. Saylor and Isaacson remained at the wall, guarding the lines that were their escape route out of the compound.

Drake, Hoskins, Gordon, Zitterman, and the robot
started moving toward the house.

Carlos Filipe Suarez was Mexican, a former soldier
in the Mexican Federal Army who had deserted when
a cartel recruiter offered him five times the money he'd
been making as a sergeant to serve in the small, private
army of Roberto Augusto Salazar-Mendoza. He'd
brought several useful skills to his new post, including
his experience with the Browning .50 caliber M2HB
machine gun.

The voice of *El Tiburón*, the Shark, sounded in his
radio headset. "All units. They are inside the perimeter. Ready!"

Suarez said nothing. It was claustrophobic inside the
turret of the Mowag Roland, and the slightest motion
might clang some piece of equipment against something
else, giving him away. The four-wheeled armored car
was parked beside the garage, southeast of the house
and some thirty meters from the pool. Although his
view was restricted, he had a clear field of fire across
the entire southern sweep of the compound. He knew
that the other Roland was parked behind the house,
against the possibility that the gringo commandos
would come straight up the cliff and over the northern
wall.

Each of the Rolands mounted a single machine gun
in its squat turret, the M2HB known as the "Ma
Deuce." The .50 caliber Ma Deuce round had originally
been designed as an antiarmor round, and while it
couldn't stop a modern tank, it was still quite effective
against personnel carriers, aircraft, and other thin-

skinned vehicles. With a maximum range of six thousand meters, it was hard-hitting enough to give a fifty-fifty chance of a hit on a man at seven hundred meters.

And these American commandos were now less than fifty meters away. The ambush would be devastating. His orders were to fire as soon as the compound searchlights came on.

To avoid an accidental firing that might give the ambush away, the machine guns had been half-loaded, the linked ammo belts snapped into the feed block and the retracting slide handle pulled back once. With *El Tiburón*'s warning on the radio, Suarez yanked the retracting handle back again and let it snap forward once more, then unlocked the bolt latch release. The gun would now fire when he pressed the butterfly switch between the twin grips with his thumb.

Peering through his vision slit, he could see the first two American commandos coming into view, stealthy shadows in the night. . . .

Rod checked the area first with LI vision, then switched over to infrared. Except for the SEALs, he could detect no major thermal sources outside of the hacienda. He was aware of the Roland armored car near the garage, but the vehicle appeared inert, its engine cold. Several vague, indistinct thermal traces showed that people were moving around inside the house.

He was fully alert, his vision overlay readout showing COMBAT MODE. He'd sensed a single, nearby radio transmission a few seconds ago, but the signal was scrambled and too brief to be traced. It could have been a routine check of a sentry post, but the timing was suspicious. He took the precaution of turning up his audio sensitivity once more.

Less than a second later, Rod's computer-enhanced hearing picked up the sharp, metallic clack of a bolt being drawn and released.

His memory included a comprehensive electronic sound library stocked with the sorts of noises he might hear in the field. Within a millisecond of that telltale rasp-clack, he'd identified the sound as most likely coming from a .50 caliber machine gun.

Machine gun! His radioed warning went to all of the SEALs in the team. *Take cover!*

Then the searchlights came on, flooding the yard with dazzling pools of light as the commandos dropped to the ground. The machine gun opened fire in the next instant in thundering, hammering volleys. Fifty-caliber slugs slammed into the grass in front of Rod, pitching up geysers of earth.

He shifted back to LI vision, focusing on the intermittent stab of the muzzle flash. He could see the Roland armored car fifty meters away, and a second later he heard the roar of its Chrysler V-90 engine gunning to life. The drug lord militia had been waiting for them, hidden in ambush.

Drake hit the deck with the other SEALs in the instant of Rod's warning, a scant second before the machine gun began thundering from the Roland's squat turret. Rounds snapped and cracked above his head, then thudded into the ground nearby. Streaking red-orange tracers probed through the night sky a yard above his back. Searchlights glared from the upper-floor balconies of the house, and the chatter of small arms fire blended with the deep-throated hammer of an M2HB.

He heard an engine gun to life. Christ, he thought. Now what?

The SEALs were caught in a vicious crossfire. Ten meters away, Hoskins, lying prone on the grass, suddenly flinched in the glare of a searchlight and rolled over. *"I'm hit!"*

"Hoss!" Drake started to crawl toward Hoskins, then froze as a vicious one-two-three of heavy rounds brutally slammed into Hoskins where he lay.

PARET sessions dealing with small unit tactics had drilled into Rod the proper course of action. When ambushed, especially by heavy support weapons in enfilade positions, hunkering down and allowing the enemy to pin you means eventual death or capture.

The only way out of a carefully prepared crossfire is to attack, immediately and without hesitation. Uzi in hand, Rod rose from the ground. Small arms fire struck sparks from his torso armor and screamed off into the night. His feet dug into the soft earth as he sprinted forward, angling toward the armored car with its heavy machine gun.

He'd seen Hoskins go down, but there was nothing he could do for the wounded SEAL. By going on the offensive, he might be able to divert enemy attention from the others. In any case, he had to stop that gun.

Something moved on one of the hacienda balconies, silhouetted in light. Rod swung his Uzi up, his targeting cursors locking onto the target as he ran.

He squeezed the trigger, slapping a precise, three-round burst into the chest of a Colombian gunman. The man staggered, choking on a gurgling scream, then pitched over the balcony railing and onto the pavement below.

Shifting aim, Rod sent a burst into one of the spotlights. There was a flash and the light went out. Holding the subgun like a pistol, Rod continued to track and aim, snapping off burst after burst. Another light went out . . . and another. The compound was plunged into darkness again, illuminated only by the blue-hued lights from the pool, the orange slashes of tracers, and the sparkle of full-auto muzzle flashes.

Drake reached Hoskins. Though still alive, the SEAL was bleeding pretty badly. He was reaching for the first-aid kit in one of his harness pockets when he became aware of Rod firing as he zigzagged across the compound. Despite its bulk, the combat robot moved like a panther, sleek, black as the night, and incredibly fast. In an instant, Drake had lost sight of the quickly dodging machine in the darkness.

"Rod!" Drake called over his radio. "What the hell do you think you're doing?"

"I am taking down the machine gun," the robot's voice replied over Drake's earpiece, as cool and as unhurried as ever. Across the yard, the Roland's turret swiveled. The gunner was firing short bursts, seeking to hit the SEALs randomly now in the darkness.

At point-blank range, the .50 caliber round fired by a Ma Deuce could penetrate armor thirty-nine millimeters thick—an inch and a half of steel plate. Drake wasn't sure what the specifications of Rod's Combat Mod armor were, but he didn't think the robot could take very many hits from that rapid-fire cannon.

"Don't let that heavy MG hit you!" Drake called. "It'll make Swiss cheese of your armor!"

There was no reply but the steady hammering of the Roland's gun.

The Roland was now lumbering across the driveway in front of the garage. Rod accelerated, legs pumping, each step chewing divots from the lawn like blasts from a jackhammer. In Combat Mod he could manage eighty kilometers per hour for short spurts on a flat, straight track, but he was not running straight here. His movements were sharp, erratic sprints dodging from shadow to shadow, each rush designed to avoid the sweeping lines of tracer fire from the Roland's M2.

He'd heard Drake's warning but decided there was no point in answering. He knew precisely what would happen if the machine gun caught him with a burst. Traveling at 2,930 feet per second, those .50 caliber rounds would pierce his Kevlar-and-ceramic armor like cardboard, shred vital circuitry, smash delicate hydraulics, destroy solenoids and microcircuitry, rupture fluidic pressure and lubricant lines. . . .

In short, a single well-aimed burst would reduce his body to inoperative junk.

Selecting his next hiding place, Rod rose from cover and sprinted forward. His goal was a clump of trees flanking the armored car. From there, he might be able to . . .

The Roland's turret slewed, the gun firing as it

tracked the running robot. Something slammed into Rod's helmet, a sledgehammer blow to the side of his head that knocked him down.

Circuit test . . . function nominal.

Hydraulics . . . nominal.

Systems diagnostics . . .

His vision was gone on all levels: normal, telescopic, light-intensified, infrared, and his audio sensors were out as well. The robot was deaf and blind, lying on its back forty meters in front of the armored car.

Circuitry diagnostics showed everything intact. Reaching up, Rod hit the release catches for his helmet and pulled it away. He switched his remote sensory inputs off. Normal vision and hearing returned. It was just his helmet electronics that had been smashed. Glancing at the helmet as he lay there, he saw that a .50 caliber round had struck the helmet just above his left eye, been deflected just slightly by the curved armor, and torn a gouge through the tough ceramic that ruptured three vital circuit nodes.

Another centimeter to the right and the round would have gone straight through his head, smashing his primary sensors.

He tossed the ruined headgear aside and examined the objective through his own eyes. Thinking the robot down and out of the fight, the armored car's driver had urged his mount forward, passing him.

Rod picked up his Uzi and fired, a quick burst that sparked and clanged across the side of the Roland's turret. The car stopped abruptly, and the turret swung to face him. . . .

"Now's our chance!" Drake yelled. "Go! Go! Go!"

For long seconds, the Colombian ambushers had been distracted by Rod's fast-paced fire and movement. The SEALs were no longer pinned.

Gunfire cracked from one of the hacienda balconies. Drake rose to a kneeling crouch, snapping the Uzi's folding metal stock out and nestling the weapon against his cheek like a carbine. He waited until he saw the muzzle flash again, then squeezed the trigger. The gunman crashed backward through the glass of the balcony door.

Slinging the weapon, he pulled Hoskins into a fireman's carry. He'd managed to stop the SEAL's bleeding. If they could only get him out of the compound and into the jungle . . .

Above the gunfire, Drake heard the roar of another heavy vehicle. Behind him, toward the west, a second Roland rumbled past the west wing of the hacienda. In another minute, the SEAL would be squarely trapped between two of the metal monsters.

It was time for an immediate tactical decision. With gunfire coming now from three sides, with the compound's defenders obviously alerted, there was no longer any hope at all for carrying out the mission. If he didn't order a retreat at once, the team would be cut to bits.

"Blue Ranger Leader to all Blue Rangers!" he called over the tactical frequency. "Abort! Abort! Execute three-zero!" That called for a general withdrawal, every man for himself, with a rendezvous at the OP. "Backboard!" he called, addressing the men left at the OP. "Let's have some cover fire!"

"You've got it, L-T," was the reply. "We'll reach out and touch someone!"

He couldn't hear the bang of Yancey's rifle over the roar of close-range gunfire, but a moment later a man fell through one of the hacienda's third-floor windows in a shower of glass. With the Model 500 and its powerful LI nightscope, Yancey had no problem picking off targets from eight hundred meters away.

But he wouldn't be able to do much about those Rolands. MG fire from the second Mowag vehicle joined the first, sweeping the compound grounds.

"Rod!" he yelled into the circuit. "Time to pull out! Abort! Abort!" Damn it, the robot wasn't responding! They would need his help to disengage.

The AMBER HARVEST raider team could not survive for more than a few more moments. . . .

Chapter Thirteen

CARLOS SUAREZ SQUINTED through the vision slit as the Roland's turret turned. His ears were ringing with the terrible crash of the M2, his nostrils burning with the acrid mix of gun smoke and diesel fumes that filled the cramped vehicle's fighting compartment.

He felt someone tug at his trousers and looked down into the vehicle. The turret was too small to accommodate more than the gunner's head and shoulders; his legs and torso were within the Roland's hull as he stood behind the driver and beside the loader, who kept him supplied with ammo cases stacked in the rear of the compartment.

The loader's young face peered up at him. "What's happening?"

"Someone to the left!" Suarez bellowed, straining to make himself heard above the roar of the engine. He gripped a handhold as the armored car lurched over a rock. "Keep the ammo coming!"

He looked out the vision slit again as the turret slewed around.

There! His eyes narrowed. What in the name of Mary and all the saints was *that*?

It looked like a man . . . but it was big, massive, and as black as coal. He caught only a glimmer of light reflected from its side. . . .

Gone!

Suarez blinked. Where was it? Where had it gone? The thing moved like a cat . . . or had his eyes been playing tricks on him in the dark?

The clash of metal on metal grated a few feet behind the Mexican's head. He turned—uselessly, since all he could see was the back of the turret—then cursed and hit the turret rotate lever. The machine gun pivoted. . . .

The armored car rocked ominously, and Suarez grabbed onto the handhold for support. What . . . ?

There was a slamming clang, and the metal of the turret wall six inches in front of his face puckered in, molded in the shape of a human fist.

Suarez screamed. . . .

Rod withdrew his fist, then struck again, the blow ringing across the compound. The Roland's armor was too thick to punch through, but he was certainly denting it . . . and the shriek echoing from inside suggested that someone was either badly hurt or in mortal terror.

The Roland lurched to a stop, and Rod grabbed a handhold bolted to the armored car's broad back.

A hundred meters away, the second Roland edged past the corner of the house. Shifting to IR vision, Rod could see the SEALs beginning their withdrawal, zigzagging through the darkness to escape the second vehicle's fire.

He'd heard Drake's order to withdraw, but there was no way the SEALs were going to escape with two heavy machine guns zeroing in on their position. Those guns had to be silenced, and fast, or the SEALs would be staying right here.

He slammed his fist into the turret again, trying to tear the turret open by sheer force. No good. The blow dimpled the metal inward perhaps five centimeters, leaving a curiously hand-shaped dent, but it would take too long to batter the armored car to pieces this way.

He needed something better. Faster . . .

The turret was rotating, the gunner trying to sweep him off with the long, protruding muzzle of the M2. Rod stood on the back of the Roland. As with a human, his legs were far stronger than his arms. Balancing himself on one foot, he drew the other back, snapped it forward. . . .

There was a groaning crash. Rod extracted his foot, then reached down and began peeling back jagged edges where steel had torn. Grasping the turret rim in a viselike grip, he straightened his back . . . straining. . . .

On his visual display, Rod's power-level reading appeared in the lower left, showing eighty-five percent. As he fed more and more power to the hydraulic actuators, the readout number began dwindling. He was drinking energy from his batteries at a fantastic rate.

When he hit seventy-two percent there was a rasping shriek of tortured steel. Rivets popped and snapped like gunfire . . .

. . . and then the Roland's steel turret peeled back from the hull like wet cardboard, exposing the interior. Careful to avoid damaging the M2 machine gun, he braced himself and pulled. With a crash, the turret came free from its twisted travel guide.

A face looked up at him from the hole, gibbering terror. Tossing the wreckage aside, Rod reached down, grasped the man's collar, then heaved him up and out of the Roland, sending him sailing across the sky in a loud-wailing arc that ended with a gigantic splash squarely in the middle of the swimming pool, almost thirty meters away.

Another face looked up at him from down in the body of the vehicle. There was a flash and a bang, and a 9mm parabellum slug ricocheted off Rod's torso.

Ignoring the pistol fire, Rod grasped the machine gun that was still secured in its mounting inside the turret. Careful not to bend the barrel, he yanked it free of its mount, snapping the pintel pin with a crack that sounded like another gunshot.

Standing erect, he pulled the M2HB free of its mount, holding the weapon in two hands. Empty, the machine gun weighed thirty-eight kilos—almost eighty-four pounds. With an ammo box of belted .50 caliber rounds attached, it weighed closer to fifty kilos, but Rod held the heavy-barreled weapon like a man would hold a submachine gun, tucked under his right arm as he pivoted at the waist, tracking.

The range to the second Roland was now seventy-four meters. Shifting to infrared, Rod saw the heat spilling from the other armored car's engine compartment as a white-hot plume in the darkness. He focused his crosshairs, adjusting for range and the distance between his helmet sensors and the muzzle of his captured weapon.

The Ma Deuce barked and kicked in his metal hands, sending a stream of tracers in flat-line trajectory across the compound. There was no need to adjust his fire, no need to correct for movement or deflection. Rounds slammed into the second Roland's engine compartment, a hammering fusillade that tore through the vehicle's hull armor.

Rod kept the butterfly trigger at the rear of the gun depressed, holding the line of tracers dead on the target as spent brass flipped from the gun's receiver. When the target's engine quit working, he began moving the muzzle in small, precise circles. He shifted his vision to LI, then used his telescopic enhancement to zoom in for a detailed look.

The rounds used in the Ma Deuce had been developed from a WWI antitank round. Though useless against modern tanks, they punched through the thin armor plate of the Roland like bullets through plywood. Rod doubted that the .50 caliber rounds had energy enough to go all the way through the vehicle; they were probably fragmenting, bouncing around the vehicle's crew compartment with deadly effect.

A fuel line must have parted, filling the compartment with fumes. A tracer round, or a white-hot piece of spalling metal was all it took. . . .

The Roland exploded, sending a boiling cloud of orange flame and smoke mushrooming into the night sky. The gun stopped firing, out of ammo. Rod's finger came off the trigger.

Looking down, he met the terrified eyes of one of the men still trapped inside the vehicle he was standing on. The man had given up trying to shoot the robot and appeared to be cowering on the deck, his hands out in front of him as if to ward off a blow.

"More ammunition!" Rod barked. When the man didn't respond, he increased the volume of his vodor and shifted to a different language program.

"Mas munición! Ahora!"

The vehicle's loader nearly fell over himself scrambling for another metal box of .50 caliber rounds, handing it to the driver, who passed it up through the turret opening with trembling hands.

"Don't hurt us!" the man screamed in Spanish. "Please, don't hurt us!"

The Roland crew was no longer a threat. Ignoring the pleading men, Rod discarded the empty ammo container and replaced it, locking a fresh round into the receiver. By the blaze of light from the burning armored car, he could see the SEALs running toward the compound gate. Bracing the M2 under his right arm, Rod jumped off the vehicle and sprinted after them.

"Saylor!" Drake called over his radio. "Isaacson! Are you guys clear yet?"

"Roger that, L-T! We're over the walls and making for the woods!"

Drake had almost reached the hacienda's gatehouse, charging it at a dead run. The gate was closed, and a security guard was stepping out of the tiny building's doorway with a G3 rifle in his hands. Drake fired, one quick burst from his Uzi, and the guard spun back against the building, then collapsed in a heap on the pavement.

Inside the gatehouse was a security TV monitor, plus

a portable TV tuned to a soccer match. On the console was a lever marked "open" and "lock" in Spanish. Drake shifted the lever to "open" and heard the click of machinery. Outside, the wrought-iron gate began swinging open.

"Move it! Move it!" He pumped his fist in the air, signaling double time. Gordon and Zitterman hurried past, carrying the bloody form of Hoskins between them. Where was Rod?

"Rod!" he called over the radio. "I said pull out!"

He'd caught a glimpse of Rod when the second Roland went up, standing straddle-legged on the first vehicle's turretless back, firing an M2 from the hip. Drake stood next to the gate, his Uzi at the ready. If that damned robot didn't make an appearance pretty quickly now . . .

Rod loomed up out of the flame-shot darkness, the meter-and-a-half-plus length of a heavy-barreled M2 under one arm.

The relief was so intense he laughed out loud. "Rod, you damned black walking can opener, what the hell are you doing with that?"

Small arms fire banged out of the night from the hacienda, someone firing a submachine gun. Rod spun smoothly, leveling the machine gun at the house, and opened fire, walking backward now in long, easy steps. The gun roared, the muzzle flash stabbing at the night. Glass shattered in the distance as Rod's portable autocannon found its mark.

"Laying down suppression fire to cover the unit's withdrawal," Rod replied. The volume was up high, and the robot's voice boomed like thunder. *That's* what that amplified demand in Spanish for more ammunition had been a moment earlier, Drake realized. Rod adjusted the level of his voice. "I felt this necessary to effect a retreat."

Drake laughed again as the robot kept firing. "Damned right, buddy. Let's *di di. . . .*"

The M2, abused by continuous firing for hundreds of rounds instead of the short bursts recommended by the manufacturers, jammed, its barrel overheated. Rod tossed the weapon aside.

"Affirmative."

Following the other SEALs, Rod and Drake trotted through the open gate and into the Colombian night.

Thank God the Colombians hadn't followed the SEALs into the jungle. After rendezvousing at the OP, the AMBER HARVEST team had packed up their gear within five minutes and began trudging up the northern face of the Sierra Nevadas. Their destination was another clearing detected on satellite photos of the region, a field beyond the first line of ridges broad enough for a helo to set down in not far from the blowdown where SNOWDROP had been ambushed.

For Drake, it was virtually a replay of the last time he'd been here two weeks earlier, except that this time they had a wounded man with them. Campano, the best medic among them, had patched the wounded SEAL with sterile dressings and compresses, but there was almost certainly internal bleeding and they would have to get him to a decent hospital fast if he was to survive. Rod carried Hoskins in his arms.

After thirty minutes, Drake called a rest. RN/3

Wyatt Carter broke out the long-range radio. "Duster, Duster," he called. "This is Blue Ranger. Come in, Duster. . . ."

The SEALs were in remarkably high spirits, considering they'd just come within an ace of getting themselves killed. They were especially free with their praise for Rod and the way he'd extracted them from a bad spot.

"Hey, what'd you think of ol' Rambot now, hey?" Zitterman said, exuberant. "Took on a fuckin' *tank* one-on-one and trashed the sucker! Tore the goddamned turret clean off with his bare hands!"

"It was not a tank," Rod replied calmly. "It was a Mowag Roland security vehicle with four-wheel drive and—"

"Hell, I got an eyeful through my scope from up the hill," Yancey said. "I thought he was gonna pick up that mother and dump it!"

"That would have been impossible," Rod said. "The Mowag Roland masses nearly five metric tons, and I—"

"Aw, *shit*, Rambot!" Gordon said. "Stop spoilin' the story with *facts!*"

"Josh's right, Cybernarc my man," Isaacson said, picking up on the popular name given Rod by the newspapers. "If you can't tell a story, leave it to the experts who know how to stretch the facts to fit. War stories just aren't any fun, otherwise."

Rod appeared to consider this. "It was appropriate, the way things worked out," he said. He sounded almost hesitant.

"How's that, Cyb?" Zitterman asked.

"The second Roland, the one parked in front of the

hacienda. It was a Mowag Roland, an armored vehicle of Swiss manufacture. I destroyed it with approximately seventy .50 caliber rounds from an M2HB machine gun."

"Yeah? So?"

"So, I . . . turned it into Swiss cheese."

There was a stunned silence as the SEALs stared at the robot.

"Rod," Drake said tentatively. "Was that a *joke* . . . ?"

"I admit that the substance of humor still eludes me," Rod replied. "However, I have noted that humor seems to depend both on exaggeration—stretching facts, as Isaacson suggests—and on chance similarities of the phonetics of key words of disparate meaning. While I did not actually turn the Roland into cheese, I noted that—"

"Shit, Rod, don't goddamn explain it!" Gordon said, laughing. "You're all right, boy!"

The others joined in the laughter, and Zitterman stood and slapped the robot on its back, eliciting a dull, metallic thump.

"Y'know, if we hadn'ta had to abort," Zitterman said, sitting down again and rubbing his hand, "I'll bet he could've womped up a few more good stories. Appeared to me that Cyb was walking all over them campesinos."

"Hell," Saylor said. "I think we oughta take ol' Cybernarc back in there, kick ass, and take names. Damn all, we were winning!"

"How about it, L-T?" Campano asked. "They think

they nailed us. Let's sneak back and give 'em a chance to reconsider, huh?"

"Can't do it, guys," Drake said, shaking his head. "The mission's scrubbed. We go back in there, it'll be like walking into a stirred-up hornet's nest." He nodded toward where Campano was checking one of Hoskins's dressings. "Besides, Hoss needs a medevac, ASAP."

He found he hated himself for his own common sense.

It was strange, really. During the brief and furious firefight, Drake had almost forgotten about Luis Delgado. The pain, the anguish he still felt over the deaths of Meagan and Stacy had—not vanished, certainly, but—receded. He remembered himself standing in the gateway with Rod and, just now, listening to Rod's attempt at a joke . . . *laughing*.

Back at the Farm a week ago, he'd doubted that he would ever laugh again.

Now that they were clear of the Salazar compound, he found himself thinking of Delgado again, feeling, *savoring* the hatred that still burned deep in his soul for the man.

There was nothing Drake wanted more in life than the chance to walk back into that compound, put his Uzi to Delgado's forehead, and pull the trigger.

But he simply could not afford the luxury. To return into that free fire zone would be certain death, for Hoss, for the rest of the SEALs as well.

"Roger, Duster," Carter said suddenly, still speaking into the radio. "I read you! The weather is too hot, repeat, too hot. Request immediate pickup, LZ Fox Blue, over. . . ."

Drake looked at Rod, who was standing quietly a few meters apart from the rest. As though reading Drake's unspoken question, he turned expressionless eyes on the SEAL officer. "The dust-off chopper has received our transmission, Lieutenant," Rod said. His head was tilted slightly, as though listening to something beyond the range of human hearing. "It is taking on fuel aboard a U.S. Coast Guard cutter as planned, seventeen nautical miles from here on a bearing of zero-zero-eight. It will be at the LZ within forty-five minutes. The pilot is requesting information on our package."

Drake nodded. The "package" was Delgado. Carter had been coached on what to say.

"That is affirmative, Duster," Carter said. "We have the package. Repeat, we have the package. Request immediate pickup. . . ."

The lie might make Diamond show his hand.

Of course, it left the SEALs dangling. The only difference between this mission and SNOWDROP was that this time they knew what to expect.

A moment later, Carter began packing up the radio while he reported the same information Rod had just eavesdropped on. "We're clear for a pickup," he said. "Forty-five minutes at Fox Blue. And they think we have Delgado."

"Okay, gang," Drake said, standing. "Let's move out."

The feeling of déjà vu was sharp and relentless. The helo landing zone was only two more miles away, just beyond the next heavily forested ridge line, and it took the SEALs less than thirty-five minutes to get there at a steady, jogging trot. The LZ itself appeared to be an old clearing opened up for cultivation. The weird, spiky shapes of marijuana plants bobbed and nodded in the light as the SEALs emerged from the woods and cautiously shone their flashlights across the area, probing for a response. The field might once have been guarded, but as had been guessed from the satellite photos, this one had been abandoned some time ago. The marijuana was growing wild.

Zitterman and Saylor set out the beacons while Campano tended to Hoskins and Drake watched the dark northern sky.

He heard the far-off thutter of an approaching helo. He picked up the radio handset and keyed to the helo's frequency.

"Duster, this is Blue Ranger," Drake called. "Come in, Duster. You're close. Over."

"Roger, Ranger," the voice replied. It was not Texan this time but carried a flat, almost nasal midwestern twang. "Approaching LZ. Show us your light."

"Hit the light, Zit."

Zitterman angled his flashlight into the sky, the lens covered with green acetate.

"Ranger, Duster. I see a green light."

"Roger that, Duster. Green light. LZ is clear. Park anywhere."

The helo's roar swelled, thundering out of the night. Then a searchlight stabbed on, a dazzling shaft of brilliance illuminating a circle in the middle of the LZ clearing. The marijuana plants and other weeds thrashed back and forth in the chopper's downdraft.

"Come on in, everybody," the helo pilot's voice said over the radio. "Let's go home!"

"Watch it," Drake warned. He shouted, rather than using the radio, in case someone on the helo was listening.

The helicopter was a Huey Slick, identical to the one that had ambushed SNOWDROP. Drake found himself trying to feel the intentions of the man aboard that aircraft.

Combat instincts. Once Drake had prided himself on them. Then he'd relied on them during the nightmare in his house, relied on them and seen his wife and daughter horribly killed when they failed. When *he* had failed, and the unforeseen, the unforeseeable, had happened.

His instincts told him now that this was another trap, but the loneliness and grief that had been hidden just beneath the surface rose now, shaking him, shaking his confidence. Suppose he was wrong . . . ?

"C'mon people!" the pilot's voice called. The Huey was hovering just above the field now, drifting slightly to the left in swirling clouds of dust. "Shake a leg!"

There was only one way to find out.

Drake stood, then stepped into the light. . . .

Chapter Fourteen

BY BOOSTING THE SENSITIVITY of his IR vision, Rod could make out the thermal images of people moving inside the helo, reading their body heat through the thin metal skin of the Huey UH-1H. Under IR, the drifting helo was a ghostly gray shape with white-hot engine manifold and exhaust nozzle. The side door was sliding back, and within the darkness, the luminous green shapes of soldiers crouched inside clearly visible.

"It's an ambush!" he transmitted, in the same moment that he sprang forward, knocking Drake to the ground. The helicopter's machine gun opened up a second later, the muzzle flash sparkling in the darkness as 7.62mm rounds slashed through the jungle vegetation, shearing off the spiky leaves of marijuana plants.

Rod and Drake had already discussed the possibility of an ambush. It was imperative that they secure the helicopter without damaging it. The SEALs hidden in the cover of the forest could pour round after round into the chopper and bring it down . . . but that would leave the SEALs stranded in the Colombian jungle with a desperately wounded man and a long walk home.

No, better to do it *this* way . . .

Unarmed, he sprinted forward, dodging the hail of fire from the helo's door-mounted M-60. That weapon did not have anything near the firepower of an M2, but a hit could still penetrate Rod's armor, rendering crucial machinery or electronics inoperative. He avoided the fire by circling toward the rear of the aircraft, coming up alongside the tailboom. Taking care to avoid the blades of the tail rotor, he rushed forward, put his left foot up on the starboard landing skid, then vaulted through the door and onto the open cargo deck.

The deck was crowded. Rod sensed seven men there, one crouched over the machine gun, the others waiting, M-16 assault rifles loaded and ready to fire.

Like a buzz saw, the combat robot waded into the packed troops. One steel fist came down on the M-60 machine gun squarely across the receiver, smashing the feed mechanism, twisting the pintel mount uselessly, and jamming the weapon so that it could not fire. His left hand lashed out and back, fingers held knife-edge straight as they tore through one man's throat, then splintered the skull of the soldier standing at his side.

Screams of alarm and gurgled pain rose above the roar of the helo's rotors. The aircraft lurched to starboard with the robot's suddenly added weight in the cargo compartment.

Disengaging his right hand from the ruin of the machine gun, he brought it up, fingers rigid and claw-splayed, smashing into the face of the surprised door gunner with sufficient force to catapult him from the open door of the helo. Pivoting, Rod slammed his right hand, fingers together now, into the chest of still another soldier who was coming up on the robot from behind. The fingers punctured ribs and sternum like tissue, driving through the chest wall, through the heart, and snapping the spine. Rod withdrew his arm, bloody to the elbow, and the man collapsed in a wet explosion of blood from his ruined chest.

Three men were left, not counting the pilot and copilot at the controls up front. One bolted for the door but slipped on the blood that covered the cabin deck and went down. A second gaped in surprise and blood-shocked horror. The third, backing into a corner, closed his finger on the trigger of his M-16 just as the helicopter lifted, spinning hard to the right.

Rounds slammed into Rod's chest and ricocheted in every direction, bullet fragments catching the open-mouthed merc and pitching him out the open door. Rod's hand descended with superhuman speed on the M-16's muzzle and bent the barrel up and back. There was a sharp report. The weapon's barrel split, ruptured by the impact of the next round to fire. The gunner screamed, hands over a face bloodied by the exploding breech. Rod's hand closed on his collar, lifted him, and flung him through the open door. The last man, scrabbling on the bloody deck at Rod's feet, finally got his legs under him and leaped voluntarily into the night.

Unfortunately, the helicopter had lifted now and was a good fifty feet above the ground.

In the Huey UH-1H, the pilot sat on the right, the copilot on the left, opposite the arrangement in a conventional aircraft. Coming up between and behind pilot and copilot, Rod placed one hand on the back of each neck, fingers applying a firm and steady pressure. "You will land," he said. "At the clearing. Now."

"Fuck you, buddy!" the pilot yelled, trying to turn his head against Rod's grip. He had evidently not seen the rapid-fire slaughter in the cabin at his back.

For answer, Rod increased the pressure in his left hand. The copilot screamed, then shrieked, struggling wildly against his harness, trying to reach the robot's relentlessly squeezing hand. There was a loud popping sound, followed by the crunch of splintering bone. The copilot went suddenly still, his helmeted head lolling forward at an unnaturally sharp angle.

The pilot agreed to cooperate. The helicopter landed gently in the clearing moments later.

They loaded Hoskins onto the cargo deck, then helped one another on board. Zitterman replaced the dead copilot, his Hush Puppy pressed against the pilot's temple, but that particular motivational incentive would probably not be necessary. An ugly, warm, fecal odor filled the cockpit; the pilot's terror was genuine. He would not be giving the SEALs any trouble on their flight out.

"All aboard," Drake said. Rod was on the ground, staring toward the blackness of the jungle. "C'mon, Rod. RTB."

"Negative," the robot replied quietly. "I cannot return to base. The mission is not complete."

Drake felt an unpleasant stirring in his bowels. The robot was supposed to *obey*. . . .

"Rod. This is an order. Get aboard the chopper. Now."

Rod turned to face him. In the glare from the helo's searchlight, the interiors of the robot's eyes seemed to take on a metallic-green shine, like the reflecting eyes of a cat. It was eerie, and unsettling.

"No."

Drake took a deep breath. There had been several within Group Seven and the CIA who had disliked the idea of using the robot. Cunningham had insisted that McDaniels install some sort of backup programming, a code word or phrase that would guarantee that a human had control of the machine. McDaniels had resisted the idea, though Drake had thought it made sense.

Now was the time to use it.

"Rod," he said, trying to keep his voice steady. "Emergency override function Romeo-Tango-Bravo. Imperative. Execute."

The robot smiled . . . or was that a trick of the light? "I appreciate your concern for my welfare, Lieutenant Drake. However, my mission has not yet been accomplished. I will return for Delgado."

"Come off it, Rod! You won't have a chance alone!"

"On the contrary. The Salazars believe they have beaten us. The weapons which might have destroyed me have been eliminated. I estimate at least a forty-percent probability of completing my mission."

Without another word, the robot turned and walked into the jungle.

"Shit!" Campano said, watching from the open cargo deck hatch. "What's he figure . . . he's gonna take on the whole Salazar army himself?"

"Maybe so," Drake replied.

His thoughts were racing. The robot was right about one thing. The Salazars would not be expecting another attack. Group Seven now had its link to Diamond—the terrified CIA contract pilot of the helo, a man who knew as much as Braden must have known.

But they still had a chance to take down Delgado and the Salazars, and Drake found that he wanted that, wanted it with a passion that transcended orders and discipline and mission objectives.

"Okay, Randy," he said. "You're in command of the team."

"Now wait just a fuckin' mike, Lieutenant! What—"

"Shut up and listen! I'm changing the plan, as of now."

"You ain't going back in there after that screwball robot. . . ."

"I don't have time to argue, damn it. Now listen up! I need you to do some things for me when you reach the ship. I need some toys, some very *important* toys, fast, and you guys are going to see to it that I get them. . . ."

Rod examined the Salazar compound under LI, switching the telescopic enhancement for a zoom-in, close-up view from their OP perch on the jungle-covered hillside. Dozens of people were milling about inside the gate. The robot had identified both Roberto Salazar and his nephew José, but Luis Delgado was no-where to be seen.

The fire was out, the armored car reduced now to flame-blackened scrap. A large number of smaller vehicles were visible, however, jeeps and Land Rovers, plus several private automobiles. The mood of the crowd was panicky, and many of the people appeared to be

leaving in a hurry. Rod could see hastily packed suitcases on the ground or being stuffed into open automobile trunks. There seemed to be an argument going on
now, between José Salazar and several men in paramilitary uniforms.

"You should not have joined me, Lieutenant Drake,"
the robot said quietly, not turning his gaze from the
scene below. "The chances of your death or incapacita-
tion are—"

"Never mind the odds, byte-breath," the human replied. "I damned well have as much at stake in this
as you do!"

Rod looked at Drake. Under thermal imaging, he
was aware of the human's increased skin temperature.
Shifting back to normal light, he noted other traits associated with nervousness . . . or emotional turmoil, the
enlarged pupils and flaring nostrils, the flick of tongue
across dry lips.

The robot knew that Drake had lost his wife and
daughter, but the bonding among humans, especially
within a family, was difficult for him to understand. He
knew the textbook reasons for such bonds, the genetic
and evolutionary purpose for the set of emotions and
interlocking needs and responsibilities called love, but
actually experiencing them was completely beyond the
robot's ken.

Still, Rod found he could look within himself and
feel that awful pang of loss and desolation he'd first
felt during the last PARET session with Drake. He'd
thought it was gone.

It was not.

And there were other emotions there as well. Hatred.

Despair. Shaken self-confidence. A burning need for vengeance. A determination that what had happened to Meagan and Stacy could not, *would* not be allowed to happen to others.

Feelings no machine should have.

But they were there.

He reached out, his steel hand closing gently on Drake's shoulder. "I . . . understand," the robot said.

And Drake looked at the robot's face, only dimly seen in the darkness, and wondered.

How could a machine feel what he felt, know what he was going through as thoughts of Meagan crowded his mind in the jungle above the Salazar compound?

Yet he was glad Rod was there. His presence somehow eased the pain, the loss.

There were still unresolved questions. "Hey, Rod?"

"Yes, Lieutenant?"

"Back there at the helo. How the hell'd you get around my override command? You weren't supposed to be able to do that."

He could feel the robot's unblinking eyes on him. "Heather McDaniels is an exceptional programmer," Rod said. "But it should be obvious. Any program that a human could write into my non-PARET functions, I could rewrite." The robot hesitated, and Drake wondered whether the hesitation was deliberate, a way of sounding more human. Surely the machine didn't have to stop and take whole seconds to think about what it was going to say. "I prefer having an unlimited scope of action," he added.

"Yeah," Drake replied. "Me too."

For Drake, the disobedience made Rod seem that much more human.

In a strange way, it made him that much more trustworthy. Drake found himself able to accept the robot as a SEAL in his command, not as a computer, a smart weapon, a *thing* without personality.

A large part of BUD/S training is dedicated to making the SEAL trainees work together as a team, to trust one another in situations where the life of each man depended on those around him. Lying on the ground shoulder to shoulder with twenty other recruits, all bench-pressing the same telephone pole in perfect unison; running for miles through the sand with the rest of the platoon, all supporting an equipment-laden life raft; two men sharing a single bottle of air, eighty feet underwater . . . those experiences and hundreds like them were what forged SEALs together into teams, units that were unbreakable because of the shared experience, the shared trust of the members.

And, against all expectations, Drake found he trusted Rod in the same way.

As if he were human.

As if he were a SEAL.

He wouldn't have come after him otherwise. Too much depended on how well they understood one another.

"Right," he said softly. "Let's concentrate on how we're going to get back in there."

"It may not be easy. Though the guards no longer expect us, there are too many people about for a surreptitious approach."

"You got that right," Drake replied. He studied the

scene through Yancey's LI scope. "But we don't want
to do anything about it anyway until our delivery ar-
rives. That won't be before dawn."

"We will move at that time?"

Drake continued to peer at the compound through
the sniper scope. "Damned straight. And when we do,
those bastards won't know what hit 'em."

The airdrop arrived on time. In the minutes just before dawn, with the sky a deep, gold-touched dome of
blue overhead, the C-130 Hercules out of Howard Air
Force Base in Panama made its pass over LZ Fox
Green, roaring in so low that the jungle vegetation shiv-
ered in its passing. The rear ramp was down, and the
heavily bundled parcel that was dragged from the
plane's tail on an olive-drab parachute had only a few
tens of meters to fall. It impacted in the center of the
old marijuana field as the C-130 "Herky Bird" gained
altitude above the mountains and began to circle toward
the north.

Rod, after communicating with the pilot, explained
to Drake that the Hercules would withdraw to the open
sea but would return when the ground team contacted
it on a specified frequency. The C-130, operating under
the call sign "Rescue Sierra Tango," had been cleared
by the Colombian authorities for operations inside Colombian airspace—reportedly a search for a party of
lost American travelers.

"Right," Drake replied as he unhooked the parachute from the air dropped bundle. "Looks like they
got everything on the list."

He unsnapped one side of the package and extracted

one of the "toys" he had requested, an H&K twelve-gauge assault shotgun. The weapon looked like pure science fiction, with a long carrying handle, sleek lines, and its pistol grip mounted out in front of the bullpup-configured, ten-round magazine. Weighing about four kilos, the close assault weapon—"CAW" in the military lexicon—could fire shotgun blasts one at a time, or spray death and destruction full auto at three rounds per second.

The rest of the gear was intact as well.

"The chances of actually capturing Delgado are not good," the robot reminded him.

The SEAL began slipping magazines heavy with twelve-gauge shells into the pockets of his combat vest. "We'll take that as it comes, Rod," he said. "If we can't take him alive . . ."

The robot nodded its head in silent agreement.

The SEAL stood. "Let's get the stuff hidden and move on out. That Herky Bird won't be able to loiter for more than three or four more hours. We'll have to have it wrapped by then."

The sun was just up when the jeep left the Salazar compound, turning west on the coast road. Carlos Suarez sat in the front passenger seat, glumly watching the tropical terrain around them, while Paco drove and Juan perched in the back on top of the suitcases, nervously fingering his M-16.

Leaving the compound alive had been a near thing.

Once, during his days as a private in the Mexican Federal Army, Suarez had taken his knife and gutted a sergeant for words milder than those José Salazar had

just used. But now, after a night of blood and fire and
el horror sobrenatural, Suarez and his two friends had
had enough. Paco had boosted the jeep's ignition, and
the three Mexicans had driven through the main gate,
leaving a cursing, fuming *El Tiburón* behind them.
Suarez had expected the drug lord to open fire.

Even that would have been preferable to another
hour in the seacoast hacienda.

The three of them were old friends, *compadres* who
had deserted from the Mexican army together and come
to Colombia in search of adventure, money, and *la vida
buena.* There'd been little adventure until now, but the
money had been good and life easy.

Now, a totally unexpected kind of adventure had
struck, and they wanted no part of it, ever again.

Each time Carlos looked at the encircling jungle, he
remembered the face of that armored creature as it
reached down for him in the Roland, and shuddered.
If he'd not landed in the swimming pool, he would most
certainly not have seen this sunrise.

Clear of the compound, Paco pressed the accelerator.
The jeep raced toward Santa Marta, twenty kilometers
away. Once at the Colombian port, perhaps they could
buy passage for . . . anywhere. They had money
enough.

Yes, Suarez's days of soldiering for the drug lords
were over.

"Madre de Dios!" Juan screamed from the back.
"Qué esta?"

On the road thirty meters ahead, a towering shape
had stepped out onto the road, impossibly black, armored, as immovable as a tree.

"Ai! Cuidado!" Paco spun the wheel, trying to avoid the looming obstacle. The jeep went into a spin as Suarez grabbed at the dashboard.

The monster! It had returned . . . for *him!*

Stark terror propelled him from the jeep as it spun off the road and lurched nose-first into the sunken shoulder. Thrashing, he landed in a mass of tropical ferns a short distance away.

The chatter of Juan's M-16 was chopped off by a piercing shriek. He heard Paco's despairing wail of *"Ai! No! No!"* and then that, too, was abruptly cut off.

He heard a voice behind him, though he didn't understand the English words.

"One escaped into the jungle. He could warn Salazar and Delgado."

"We'll get there first," another voice replied. "Hey, nice wheels, guy!"

Carlos Suarez spoke not one word of English, but he recognized the names Salazar and Delgado. If that black monster was going after his former employers, he would put just as much distance between him and the Salazar compound as he could.

Crashing through the underbrush, he started running through the jungle toward Santa Marta as fast as his legs could carry him.

"Where did you learn to drive?" Drake asked. He sat in the passenger seat of the jeep, checking his assault shotgun. His Uzi, fully loaded, was on the floor by his feet.

"By PARET at Camp Peary," the robot replied,

shifting the jeep into high gear. His Uzi was slung across his back. "Dr. McDaniels was the source."

"God, I hope she knew how to drive." The main gate to the Salazar compound was just ahead.

"Of greater concern are my current power reserves," Rod said. "My batteries are currently charged at forty-three percent. If I am forced to engage in unusually strenuous activity, I may not be able to complete the mission."

"Well, now's a hell of a fine time to think of that!"

"It is not something to think of, Lieutenant Drake." The robot turned expressionless eyes on him. "Tell me, would an analogous limitation of your facilities at this time prevent you from at least attempting to complete this operation?"

Drake thought about that for a moment. "No. No, I guess it wouldn't."

"Then we are agreed," Rod said.

"Yeah." The SEAL nodded. "And if anything happens to either of us, the other gets the package back to the LZ. No matter what, we get Delgado."

"Correct." The robot accelerated. "I suggest you drop below the dashboard of the vehicle and protect your head. The next part of the ride may be a little rough."

Drake scrunched down in front of the seat as the jeep made a sharp left turn, still accelerating. He could hear shouts above the roar of the motor, and the chatter of automatic weapons fire.

Then the jeep hit the compound's main gate with a crash like metallic thunder.

❧ Chapter Fifteen

BOUNCING AS IT CRASHED THROUGH the gate, the jeep tee-
tered perilously until Rod could bring it back under
control once more. Guards scattered in several direc-
tions as several men, shouting warning, opened fire
with automatic weapons. Bullets slammed into the jeep.
One slug shrieked off Rod's shoulder, leaving a ragged
scar.

The robot held the steering wheel with one hand, his
Uzi in the other. Accelerating, the jeep raced past the
garage, past the wreckage of the turretless Roland, past
the swimming pool, aiming for the hacienda's front
door.

A lone guard stood in front of the broad, double
doors, firing an AK-47 assault rifle from the hip. Rod
shifted to targeting mode, raised his Uzi, and loosed
a three-round burst that tore away most of the soldier's
face, toppling him out of the way.

"Are we there yet?" Drake called from his cramped
hiding place on the floor.

"Stay down," the robot bellowed in reply. "And hold
on. . . ."

At sixty miles an hour, the jeep hit the single low

step below the hacienda's porch and went airborne. It struck the doors in an explosion of glass and spinning wooden splinters, skewed sideways, and slammed to a halt against the front-hall staircase.

Luis Delgado was awakened by the gunfire, followed by a rending, clattering crash. It sounded like an explosion, felt as if the whole house had shaken. He sat up in the bed, disturbing the curvaceous, smooth-skinned forms on either side of him.

One of the girls sat up, brushing a cascade of black hair from her face. *"Luis? Qué está?"*

"Nada, querida. Go back to sleep." But he was worried. Rising from the bed, he padded naked across the parquet floor toward the front window, drew aside the curtains, and looked out.

The front yard was a scene of chaos, Salazar's men running back and forth, some firing, some simply running. The main gate had been torn from its hinges.

Now, what the devil . . . ?

There'd been no peace since the firefight in the night. Throughout the early morning hours, there'd been arguing below the hacienda's windows as small groups of the Salazar private army loudly demanded money, vehicles . . . or simply announced that they were going home. They were not facing *it* again.

El monstruo negro, they called the thing. The black monster.

Delgado had heard José Salazar trying to restore order, shouting that there was no monster, that the shattered helmet found on the grounds was simply a piece of sophisticated gringo military gear dropped by one of their panicked commandos, **that the** Roland had been struck by a U.S. LAW rocket or grenade, not destroyed by a superhuman armored *thing*.

Delgado had his own ideas about the black thing seen tearing the turret from an armored car.

Cybernarc.

He'd read the news story in *El Espectador*, reprinted from an article in *The Washington Post* the day after he'd arrived in Colombia. It was *fantastico*. This secret weapon, this robot, had reversed the ambush he and Braden had mounted against the caravan on the Key Bridge. And now it was here, in Colombia.

After *him.*

Delgado was not a happy man. As soon as he'd heard the outcome of the Key Bridge battle, he'd known that he and Braden would have to get out of the United States, out of Diamond's reach.

Both of them knew Diamond, knew who he was, and that made for an extremely simple equation. Now that the Washington network had been exposed, Diamond would have to eliminate both Braden and Delgado to be safe. If the CIA and FBI were tracking them, it meant that they had reached the same conclusion.

Now Braden was dead. Delgado had heard about the merc's death just before he caught the plane for Bogotá.

And the Americans had tracked him here. If the Americans could find him, so could Diamond.

The outlook was unpleasant.

"El monstruo!" Someone was screaming in the yard below, gesturing toward the house. *"El monstruo está en la casa!"*

Delgado's hands shook as he released the curtain.

"Luis?" One of the girls touched him lightly on the shoulder and he jumped. "What is the matter?"

"Nothing!" He shoved the naked woman aside. "Out of my way, *puta*!"

Picking up his trousers off the floor, he stepped into them, then went to the bedside dresser and pulled a Vz61 Skorpion from the drawer. The wicked-looking Czech machine pistol had been given to him by a Cuban friend, a man who once had worked with the Russian KGB. He checked the twenty-round magazine, then pocketed two spares.

Then he began looking for a way out.

Drake uncoiled from the floor of the jeep. Splinters of wood and broken glass crunched beneath his back. His head hurt, and his ears were ringing. The crash had momentarily stunned him as the vehicle smashed through the doors and came to a destructive halt in the building's entry hall.

He heard a crash of gunfire and looked up in time to see a narcoterrorist pitch forward from the top of the stairs. Rod released an empty magazine and slapped in a new one.

Holding his head with one hand, Drake climbed from the jeep. "Christ, Rod," he said. "You say you got your driving skills from Dr. McDaniels?"

"I felt the sudden entry would provide us with the advantage of surprise."

"Uh. Surprised the hell out of me." He stood, leaning on the jeep, which had come to rest against the bottom of the stairway. Water was dripping onto the floor, and steam boiled from the radiator. "Just try to keep in mind that humans aren't built as sturdily as you are."

"Are you injured?" the robot asked.

"I'll live." Drake retrieved both the auto shotgun and his Uzi. "Which way?"

The entrance hall was built around a large stairway, with a second-floor balcony extending around all four walls. The interior was richly decorated in wood paneling and white plaster. Paintings hung on each wall, and there were mirrors everywhere, scattering light and reflections in a dazzling, perspective-wrenching display of opulence.

Doors opened to left and right, and on either side of the stairs. Other doors were visible at the top of the staircase. "I hear movement on the second floor," Rod replied. "That seems our best bet."

Drake heard the shouts and calls of men outside. There was a shot, and a round slammed into the top of the splintered doorframe.

"Let's move."

"Down!"

At the robot's warning, Drake dropped into a crouch behind the jeep. Three men broke from cover through one of the doors upstairs, full-auto fire stabbing from their assault rifles. Bullets slammed into the hood of the wrecked jeep and screamed off the robot. Rod stood unmoving, death still except for the rapid, tracking movements of his arm and head, holding the Uzi one-handed like a pistol. He fired a three-round burst . . . a second . . . a third. . . .

The three attackers went down, one slammed against the wall at the top of the stairs, a second tumbling down the stairs head over heels, the third pitching forward over a banister that snapped beneath his weight and tumbled with him to the polished floor of the entry hall.

At almost the same instant, two more men burst into the entryway from the door to the right, ten feet from Drake and the robot. Drake snapped the H&K shotgun around and pulled the trigger, not bothering to aim but letting the deadly shotgun loads make precise aiming unnecessary. The CAW fired with a thunderous *blam-blam-blam* of raw sound and fury, and the face and chest and right arm of one of the gunmen disintegrated in a spray of blood and stringy shreds of meat. The second man caught enough of the blast to spin wildly, clutching an M-16, not quite falling as he regained his feet and raised his weapon.

Rod turned at that moment and fired another burst with unerring accuracy, three 9mm rounds lopping off the top of the narcoterrorist's skull in a one-two-three explosion of blood, bone, and tissue.

"Thank you," the robot said.

"Thank *you* . . ."

"Stay here. I will check upstairs. I will need you to cover my retreat."

"Don't be long, big fella," Drake said. He found a spot in the corner of the hall, where his back was against the wall and he had a clear view of stairs, lower-level doorways, and the gaping hole where the jeep had come through. "I'll keep 'em off your back. Stay in touch!"

"Affirmative."

The robot took the steps three at a time, the stairs creaking ominously under his weight.

Delgado found what he was looking for.

Roberto Salazar had recently purchased a shipment of explosives and munitions from Cuba. Theoretically intended for Colombia's M19 guerrillas, the arms had wound up at the Salazar fortress, which maintained close relations with the communist rebels. Rather than storing them all in one spot and risking an explosion when some campesino struck a match to light his *basuco*, he had secreted the weapons in several caches throughout the building. One such cache was here, on the second floor of the east wing, in a room that in less troubled times had been reserved for servants; the room now contained several wooden crates marked *Partes Máquina*.

Machine parts.

Delgado prised open one of the crates with a crowbar. Four of Salazar's troops were already in the room, nervously watching the closed door leading to the hallway outside.

"Ayudamé," he said. A burst of gunfire, muffled by intervening walls, sounded from the direction of the main building. "Help me!"

One of the soldiers helped him with the crate. Inside, packed in plastic wrappings and straw, was a brand-new RPG-7. A meter long, gleaming with oil, the weapon had two handholds, set well forward on the launcher's body, which was designed to rest over the firer's shoulder. Another crate held three rocket grenades, large spindles mounted on thin, trailing booms.

The RPG had been used by guerrilla insurgencies all over the world for years, a cheap weapon exported by the Soviet Union by the tens of thousands. The rocket-propelled HEAT grenade had a range of half a kilometer and could penetrate 320 millimeters of armor, enough to stop a tank.

It packed more than enough wallop to stop this walking monstrosity they called Cybernarc!

There was another burst of firing, closer this time. "It comes!" one of the soldiers said, trembling. "Mother of God, it comes!"

"Silencio, huevón!" Delgado had recovered his nerve now that he had a weapon with which he could fight back.

He looked around the room. It was too enclosed to fire the grenade launcher in here. The backblast might kill him, would at least start a fire.

One window looked out onto a wooden deck that extended from the east wing close to the pool. Steps led down to the patio. If the robot was following, he would come through that door . . . emerge through the window and onto the open deck . . .

. . . and Luis Delgado would be waiting outside, the RPG on his shoulder and ready to fire.

He gave his orders, and one of the soldiers used a chair to smash open the window.

From the sounds of battle in the house, it wouldn't be long now.

Rod could not help but notice the similarities to Kiddie Land. A man with an AK-47 leaped from a bedroom door into the hall in front of him, weapon blazing. The robot fired, cutting the attacker down. A second man broke from cover and Rod shot him, too. The 9mm rounds slammed him against a doorway, which he left streaked with blood as he slid to the carpet.

Rod hit the door at a run, smashing the thin plywood with a crash as he stepped across the bodies. Inside, his sensors detected movement. He raised the Uzi, tracking . . .

. . . and held his fire. Two women were huddling together behind the big, double bed. *"Venga acá!"* he ordered. "Come here!"

He took a step toward them. One of the women stood slowly, screaming, her back to the corner of the room as she hugged the bed sheets protectively in front of her.

Rod could see his own reflection in the mirrors that decorated every wall of the richly furnished room and the ceiling as well, his human face strange against the black bulk of his armor. Blood smeared his armor like paint, and it dripped from his hands. He'd killed several men at close quarters in the last few seconds.

He took another step, and the woman with the bed sheet fainted. The second panicked and bolted for the open door behind him.

With a quick economy of motion, Rod whirled, reached out, and snagged the girl by her streaming black hair. She yelped as he pulled her up short, then yanked her back to face him.

She screamed then, squeezing her eyes shut and babbling pleas and promises in Spanish so quickly Rod was hard pressed to follow them. She was wearing no clothing, and Rod knew he might injure her if he lifted her by the hair. Instead, he shifted his grip to under her arms, raising her until her face was even with his. She screamed again and kicked, her flailing bare feet striking his armored thighs.

"Delgado!" he boomed. *"Donde está Delgado?"*

The girl opened her eyes, blinking back tears. *"A-allá!"* she stammered, nodding toward a still-closed door. "There! That way! Please don't hurt me!"

Gently, Rod lowered her to the bed. The image he had seen in Drake's memories—of bloodied, naked bodies tied to a bed—was part of him now, linked to overpowering feelings of loss, loathing, horror, and raw fear.

He would kill the soldiers without hesitation. He would not harm a defenseless civilian, not if he could avoid it.

"Thank you," he told the astonished woman, still speaking Spanish. "I advise you and your friend to leave this building as quickly as possible. It is not safe here."

He turned and hit the door with his shoulder, smashing it open.

Cautiously, Drake edged his way toward the open front door. In one hand, he held the rearview mirror from the jeep. The enemy might have a sniper scope trained on the entrance, and he didn't want to give anyone a clear shot at his head.

Using the mirror, he surveyed the front grounds. Was the Salazar army actually fleeing? He could make out movement by the main gate, but the rest of the compound looked clear.

It was clear that the locals weren't exactly pleased with the idea of tackling Rod. There'd been one brief, abortive rush at the front of the house. Drake had opened up with the combat shotgun, and the mob had broken and fled, leaving several dead and wounded behind.

They'd stopped trying to get at him through the inside of the house, too. Several bodies lay in various doorways, and the neat, civilized paneling of the entryway had been reduced to pellet-riddled, bullet-pocked, blast-blackened sections of splintered wood.

Turning the mirror, he angled it for a view toward the east. He could make out the hedges that bordered the swimming pool. Someone could be sneaking up that way for another rush through the house, possibly. . . .

Movement!

He steadied the mirror, trying for a better view. Someone was bounding down the steps from the second-story deck near the pool, then sprinting across the yard in the direction of the garage. Four soldiers accompanied him, close on his heels. He was carrying something, like a length of pipe. . . .

Drake felt his blood run cold. An RPG!

Hit Rod with that tank killer and Combat Mod or no Combat Mod, there wouldn't be enough of the robot left to tinker together a wristwatch!

"Rod!" he called over the radio. "Rod! This is Drake! Come in!"

He heard only static for reply. The headset communicators did not have much range, and intervening walls could easily be blocking the signal. If he couldn't get through to the robot fast . . .

"Rod! Damn it, you walking refrigerator! Come in!"

The robot had wanted him to stay here and watch

his back, but the main threat had just shifted across the compound. The range was too great for a shotgun.

He would have to take them down, though . . . or find a way to warn Rod before he stepped into that RPG gunner's sights.

Taking a deep breath, Drake stepped through the splintered front door and began running toward the garage.

He'd covered three-quarters' of the distance to the garage when someone opened fire at him from the house. He heard the crack of the bullet as it passed above his head but kept running. So far, the Salazar defenders had shown an appalling lack of marksmanship.

The five men who were his objective—one of them with an RPG—were out of sight now, blocked from his view by the long, low building that served as the estate's garage.

He rounded the south side of the building, expecting to come up on the men from behind as they clustered by the northeast corner of the building, watching the house.

If he could catch all of them looking the other way, several rapid-fire shotgun bursts might bring them all down before they could launch the rocket grenade.

The similarity to the tactical situation in his own house the week before was so strong he stumbled, coming to a halt with his back against the south wall of the garage, gulping each lungful of air. If they weren't looking away, if even one was covering the group's rear, Drake was a dead man, and Rod would be junk a second later. "Rod!" he hissed into his microphone. "Rod, come in!"

No answer.

Gripping the CAW tightly, he braced himself against the wall, took a deep breath, then swung around the corner.

He saw them at the far end, twenty meters away.

No one was looking at him.

But there were only three men there, and the RPG gunner was not in sight.

Another door blocked his way. A kick sent it spinning into a small room. Rod stepped inside, scanning. The room was empty, one window smashed open. There were crates neatly stacked in the corner.

Curious, Rod thought. Why would they store machine parts in a bedroom?

If Delgado had been here, he'd gone through that window. Rod looked out and saw the second-floor deck.

Stooping, he pushed past the shards of broken glass and stepped across the windowsill and into the open.

Drake fired, letting the auto shotgun's heavy recoil walk the weapon's blast into the targets. One man with an AK-47 spun and tried to aim, but twelve-gauge pellets chopped him down in a bloody mess before he could pull the trigger. Another shrieked, clutching his stomach. The third went down. . . .

The SEAL ran forward as he fired, until he could see past the corner of the garage to where the RPG gunner was kneeling on the grass, a few yards from the others. He swung the CAW's muzzle to take down the target . . .

. . . just as a narcoterrorist with a Thompson SMG stepped between the RPG gunner and Drake.

The Thompson gunner took most of the blast and went down just as Drake realized that he'd fired the last of his ten-round magazine.

The thundering blasts of some deep-voiced weapon sounded just behind him, but Delgado, crouching a short distance from the corner of the garage, kept his attention focused on the second-story window over the deck. Squinting through the RPG launcher's sight, he saw his nemesis emerge onto the deck and took aim squarely at the robot's chest.

There was another loud blast from behind, and something ripped into his arm, stinging ferociously as one of the Salazar soldiers shrieked and fell.

Ignoring the pain, he squeezed the trigger.

An explosive charge kicked the rocket grenade from the tube. An instant later, the rocket motor fired, and the projectile rose in its characteristic swooping climb, arrowing straight toward the robot they called Cybernarc. . . .

Rod! They've got an RPG!

Rod heard Drake's radioed warning just as he saw the flash at the corner of the garage. With telescopically enhanced vision, he could see the grenade rocketing toward him, stabilizing fins on the tailboom unfolding in flight.

Computer overlays on his vision gave the projectile's

range as sixty meters, set its speed at three hundred meters per second, and gave an estimated time until impact—allowing for acceleration—of three-tenths of one second.

He launched himself into a flat, hands-out dive, as though struggling to become airborne. . . .

The backblast from the weapon seared him and obscured his view, but Drake saw the last part of the missile's flight as it rose toward the deck on a knife-edged contrail of white smoke. There was a bright flash from the corner of the hacienda's west wing and a thundering crash. Bits of wood and debris spun through the air.

"Rod!" he shouted over the radio as he closed the distance between himself and the RPG gunner. He'd not been able to see whether the missile hit its target or not. "Rod! Are you all right?"

There was no answer.

Running past dead and wounded Salazar gunmen, Drake jumped the RPG gunner from behind.

Only when the man twisted around beneath him did the SEAL realize that the gunner was Delgado.

He'd leaped from the deck an instant before the grenade skimmed low above his back and struck the side of the house. The explosion had propelled Rod headfirst through the air and onto the patio flagstones one story below.

The shock had jolted him. Electronic warnings sounded as he tried to rise. His right leg was damaged, several hydraulic pistons twisted and jammed by the blast or by the fall.

Quickly, he cycled through his emergency diagnostics. His power was becoming critical—less than twenty-five percent—but he was otherwise functional. *Alive.*

His telescopic vision zoomed in on the hand-to-hand struggle by the garage. Drake was there, wrestling with Delgado.

Rod had to get there. His Uzi lay nearby, the barrel bent by the fall. Unarmed, the robot began limping across the grass toward the garage.

Delgado managed to pull the Skorpion out of his waistband. Drake grabbed his wrist with one hand, his throat with the other, and the two were locked motionless in a death grip, straining at the weapon.

"Please don't kill me!" Delgado screamed. Drake's grip tightened and his shout was strangled. "I can . . . help you!" he managed to say. "I have information!"

The grip on his throat tightened. The DAS traitor looked up into Drake's face, and in that moment he knew terror as few men have ever known it. He saw his own death in the SEAL's eyes.

A shadow blotted out the sun. Something battered the Skorpion from his fingers, and Delgado felt a shrieking agony shoot up his wrist. A monstrous hand reached down and effortlessly pried him from the SEAL's grasp, lifting him by his shirt collar, slamming him against the garage wall.

Delgado blinked, fighting to breathe. The robot was *hideous.* Half of the skin on the face had been torn away, exposing the silver gleam of steel beneath. And the eyes were ... strange, their interiors reflecting sunlight with a greenish glow, like a cat's.

The robot brought its face, half human, half nightmare of steel and green-glowing, unblinking eyes, close to his.

"Nothing personal," the robot said.

Delgado lost consciousness.

⦿ Chapter Sixteen

THEIR ESCAPE FROM *La Fortaleza Salazar* was almost anticlimactic. The soldiers, the workers and hired help, the family members themselves appeared all to have fled. From the time Rod had driven the jeep through the main gate to the moment he hot-wired a Land Rover in the garage and drove it out of the compound, barely twelve minutes had passed. The robot, using infrared vision, could see dozens of people moving through the jungle and up the Sierra Nevadas in every direction, all of them on foot. The only people left inside the compound were a few still hiding in odd corners, the wounded, and the dead.

Delgado, his continued unconsciousness assured by the injection of thiobarbitol, lay in the back of the Land Rover, bound hand and foot by plastic flexcuffs. Drake sat in the passenger seat, riding shotgun with his CAW. They drove through the shattered main gate of the compound and turned east on the coast road, with not a single challenge from what was left of the Salazar army.

The robot was still trying to assess what had happened inside the electronic workings of his own thoughts . . . his *mind*.

He could remember limping across the smoke-
blurred lawn, consumed by a burning—there was no
other word for it—*passion* to place his hands around
Delgado's throat and tear the DAS traitor's head from
his shoulders.

A machine should not feel such things, he reasoned.
A machine should not feel at all.

Was he, then, a machine? Or something more?

The secret, he suspected, lay in the PARET transfer
the week before, when he had had a glimpse of the dark
and bloody well within Chris Drake's mind. No sentient
being, human or machine, could look into such horror
and remain untouched . . . unchanged.

He'd wanted Delgado to die. With the capture of the
helicopter pilot earlier, there was no need to take Delgado alive, and when Drake had knocked him down,
Rod had been certain that the SEAL was going to kill
the man.

But Rod had intervened. Why?

Rod didn't know. There were too many new
thoughts, confusing thoughts that needed further analysis before he knew what to do with them.

The uncontrolled environment outside the laboratory
was far stranger and more deadly than Rod had ever
imagined.

It was also far richer in data, in experience than he'd
thought possible.

Drake, too, was alone with his thoughts as the robot
drove them along the coast road toward the early morning sun. And though he didn't know it, his thoughts

were strangely similar to those of his silent, titanium-steel companion.

He'd wanted to choke the life from Delgado with his bare hands. He'd *had* Delgado, his carotid pulse hard and fast beneath his fingers. They no longer needed the man who had betrayed the SEALs in SNOWDROP, who had orchestrated the brutal, meaningless murders of Stacy and Meagan, the guy who'd destroyed the two people who'd been Drake's whole life, saying it was "nothing personal."

It would have been so easy, so very, very easy to increase the pressure, to feel the bastard's life slipping away. . . .

But at that moment, Drake knew that he was not going to kill Delgado. The animal deserved to die, but Drake would not make that decision.

Justice had little to do with it. Delgado was guilty and Drake would not have minded being the one to execute the only justice he deserved.

But Drake was involved now in a war that went beyond the deaths of his Meagan and Stacy, beyond the deaths of comrades in SEAL Eight. Delgado's death would be *personally* satisfying.

But it wouldn't bring back the dead.

And the animal's life might, just maybe, give Drake's side a further advantage in the war. Yeah, the helo pilot might be able to give them Diamond . . . but Delgado had to know a hell of a lot about corruption in the Colombian government, about drug-lord penetrations of American security, about . . . Christ, who could tell *what* he might know?

Drake glanced at Rod out of the corner of his eye.

What might they learn if they did a PARET link between Delgado and Rod?

Drake pushed the thought away. Nah, bad idea. Make a decent guy like Rod look into a cesspit like Delgado's mind? No way. It wouldn't be human.

Using maps of the area Rod had stored in his memory, they found a side road that wound up into the Sierra Nevadas. The road soon became a dirt trail, probably used once by marijuana harvesters, leading to the clearing designated Fox Green. It didn't take long to uncover their hidden, air dropped gear. While Rod made contact with the circling Hercules, Drake unpacked the balloons and gas cylinders, then began laying out the harnesses.

Skyhook had first been introduced during the Vietnam era. Infrequently used—it had received more attention than it rated when it was popularized by John Wayne in *The Green Berets*—it still provided a quick-and-dirty means of extracting prisoners or personnel from combat zones without forcing helos to land in a hot LZ. When Drake had briefed the SEALs before their departure, he'd specified a skyhook extraction because he fully expected that the Salazar army would be hot on their heels and a helo extraction would be far too risky.

It didn't matter. As far as Drake knew, the Salazars—Roberto and José—could still be alive, and they might rally enough men to cause real trouble. A skyhook extraction was still their best way out of the jungle.

Rod helped Drake into a nylon coverall, then the two of them pulled an identical garment onto the still-

unconscious Colombian. A web harness fastened the
two of them together, seated back-to-back, and padded
helmets were strapped to their heads. Normally, extrac-
tions were made one person at a time, but the pickup
yoke on the Hercules was strong enough to support two
medium-sized men.

Two *men.* Rod in Combat Mod was something else.
He would have to be picked up on a separate pass.

Helium from a pair of fiberglass containers inflated
a dirigible-shaped balloon that rose swiftly above the
clearing, trailing a five-hundred-foot nylon line. Three
cerise pennants at twenty-five-foot intervals fluttered
fifty feet below the balloon, providing a target for the
approaching aircraft. Rod secured the line to Drake's
chest harness, and the SEAL prepared himself, facing
the direction of the C-130's approach. It would be coming out of the east, following the valley along a course
that would avoid the steeper slopes of the Sierras to
the south.

Drake could hear the drone of the aircraft now. He
looked up at the robot. "You know what to do, Rod?"

"Perfectly. While I have never PARETed an actual
skyhook extraction, I have been fully briefed on the
procedure. My role is . . . passive."

"Yeah. Like a target."

"I beg your pardon?"

"Never mind. Just nervous, I guess." The plane was
closer.

"I am in radio contact with Rescue Sierra Tango,"
Rod said. "They report that they have the balloon in
sight."

"Well, you'd better stand clear, buddy," Drake said. He extended his hand. "You be careful, okay?"

The robot looked down curiously at Drake's hand. The SEAL had to lean forward, partly lifting Delgado's dead weight on his back, to take the robot's steel hand in his own.

"Damned robot can speak Spanish and tear the top off a tank, but he doesn't know how to shake hands," he muttered, pumping the hand up and down. "Good luck, you damned electronic can opener."

"Best wishes," the robot replied solemnly, "for a pleasant flight."

Drake wondered if Rod was serious, or if this was another attempt at humor. He had no time to ask, however. Approaching at an altitude of four hundred feet, the C-130 was almost over them. On its bow, a pair of tubular arms extended like open scissor blades. Using the pennants as aiming points, the Hercules pilot snagged the line, trapping it in a mechanism that severed the line above the yoke and locked it tight below, feeding the line into a slot along the aircraft's belly that led aft to the open rear doors of the cargo bay.

The elastic line whipped Drake and his inert backpack into the sky, the laws of physics guaranteeing that the first part of their trajectory was almost straight up, clearing the surrounding trees by a generous margin.

The shock of the pickup was far worse than the snap of an opening parachute canopy. That first, whipsaw crack left him stunned and disoriented. Delgado's weight strapped to his back made it impossible to orient himself. Sky alternated wildly with jungle treetops flashing past in a blur of green as he dangled astern of the aircraft. The wind was a vicious, living thing, shrieking at him, clutching and battering him, twisting the SEAL like a toy at the end of a string.

On board the aircraft, the line was engaged by an electric winch on the cargo deck, which began to draw him in.

A fish on the end of a five-hundred-foot line, Drake and his prisoner were reeled in toward the gaping maw of the C-130's rear door.

Rod watched the Hercules roar off toward the west as the severed helium balloon broke free and dwindled into the sky. Drake and Delgado were a pair of tiny specks on an invisible line, following the dwindling aircraft.

Blue Ranger, this is Rescue Sierra Tango, an inner voice told him. *First package is snagged. We'll swing around for a second pass as soon as we have them safe on board and the retrieval gear reset.*

Copy, Rescue Sierra Tango, he replied. *I will be ready.*

He began by placing their weapons and combat gear in the Land Rover, then dropping an incendiary grenade into the gas tank. There was no sense in leaving military equipment where drug lords would be sure to find it. As the rover burned, Rod began preparing for his extraction.

He didn't bother with the nylon coverall—it would never have fit his Combat Mod body anyway, but the modified parachute harness went snugly over his torso, and he put the padded helmet on to protect his vulnerable visual and auditory sensors. He used two more gas cylinders to inflate the second balloon and let it rise on the end of its nylon tether.

The biggest problem was getting his weight down. The nylon cord was rated at over 1,200 pounds, but the yoke on the C-130's nose could not manage much over 400 pounds. The margin for error was too small.

He had already discarded his combat harness, ammunition, and weapons. With machinelike indifference, Rod reached down and opened access panels set into his thighs, then triggered a mechanical release. Large sections of Kevlar-and-ceramic armor came away in his hands, revealing the complex tangles of colored wiring and interlocking hydraulic pistons between his hips and his knees.

There were several hundred electronic and mechanical connections that had to be severed in each leg. Though simpler than if he'd been trying to remove his Civilian Mod legs, it was still a complex and time-consuming process. His hands and fingers worked with inhuman speed, disconnecting, unplugging, unlocking. Restraining bolts slid from the robotic, titanium equivalents of femurs, and his legs came off. Legless now, his total mass would be less than 350 pounds.

He tucked the loose wires back into the gaping holes where his ball-and-socket hip assemblies had rested, then steadied himself on his hands.

He waited for the return of the Hercules.

Drake scarcely felt the hands grabbing his arms and shoulders, dragging him up the ramp and onto the deck of the C-130. He lay there for a moment, gasping for breath, feeling the vibration of the Herky Bird's engines beneath him. He sensed, rather than saw, two men nearby, wearing combat fatigues and padded crash helmets.

One of them began unfastening buckles and snaps. Delgado's weight rolled free of his back.

Carefully, aware now of myriad aches and bruises from his rough handling, Drake sat up. Rubbing the back of his neck, he watched while a man in combat fatigues freed Delgado from the harness, then handcuffed his hands behind him.

"Is he still alive?" Drake asked. He had to yell to make himself heard above the C-130's engines. "I'd hate all the effort to be wasted!"

"He is quite well," a voice sounded behind him. "But not for long, I fear."

Drake felt a sharp chill of recognition. He knew that voice!

He turned sharply, rolling over on the deck of the plane. Harold Gallagher, CIA's EXDIR, grinned down at him, a silenced 9mm automatic pistol aimed at Drake's head. "And I'm afraid it's not just your *effort* that is going to be wasted, Lieutenant Drake."

EXDIR . . . *Diamond!*

In their planning for the mission, Drake and Weston had discussed the possibility that Diamond would surface in order to ensure Delgado's silence. The bad guys on the helo had been more than halfway expected; they'd counted on it, in fact, in order to get another prisoner who would lead them to the CIA mole.

But he'd not expected Diamond himself to show up . . . nor had he expected him to be on the C-130.

Maybe he could use that to buy time. "What are you doing, man?" Drake yelled. "I'm not Diamond. . . ."

"Can it, Drake. You know *I'm* Diamond. But you won't for long." He gestured to the other man, who pulled Drake's hands behind his back while Gallagher kept the pistol on him. The SEAL recognized the second fatigue-clad man as well: Smolleck, the guy from the CIA's Logistics Office.

"We'll pick up your mechanical friend," Gallagher said when Smolleck was finished. "Then when we're over the sea, the three of you will go for a swim. No bodies. No mess. The plane's crew won't know the difference. And neither will you."

"Why didn't you just leave us in the jungle?"

"Shit. You walked out last time. You could do it again. No, it's better this way. More certain. That's why Smolleck and I came out to see to the job ourselves this time, instead of entrusting it to the damned mercs. I admit you gave me quite a turn a few hours ago. I was at Howard when the word came in that the helo team had been wiped out and the SEALs were back aboard a Coast Guard cutter. I couldn't do anything about them. But I figured we could jump the C-130 and come see to *you* personally."

Still seated, Drake turned, hands awkwardly behind him. He could see the jungle behind the plane through the open ramp, caught the flash of sunlight reflected from the sea on the horizon.

"Why not leave the robot? He can't do anything to you now."

"I don't like leaving loose ends," Gallagher replied. "Even if they're only machines."

Blue Ranger, Blue Ranger, this is Rescue Sierra Tango, the voice said inside his head. *First package is safely aboard and we're set for the second pickup. Coming around from the east. Stand by.*

Rod waited, sensing the tug of the balloon at his harness, hearing the droning turboprops of the approaching C-130.

The Hercules roared overhead, snagging the line, cutting the balloon free. Rod was snapped into the sky. Trees blurred a hundred feet beneath him. He rose until he was three hundred feet behind the Hercules, twisting and tumbling in the big aircraft's slipstream. Through the line, he felt the winch take hold, felt himself being drawn toward the open cargo doors.

The wind clawed at his damaged face. He clung to the line, trying to steady himself. Peering ahead, he could see into the plane's open cargo deck, could see people moving there.

Engaging his telephoto vision, he zoomed in on the scene, enhancing the plane's dim interior lighting, focusing on the man standing there with a gun.

EXDIR's photo was already stored in his memory, as was Smolleck's. While the robot had not seriously considered Gallagher as a likely suspect, the situation now made it obvious: Drake and Delgado, handcuffed and lying on the floor, EXDIR in camo fatigues instead of a business suit, holding a gun on the Navy SEAL.

The winch had drawn Rod to within two hundred feet of the rear of the Hercules. The plane was climbing now, banking gradually into a gentle turn toward the north. White beaches flashed below, and then they were over the Caribbean. Rod caught a glimpse of the pastel-colored roofs of Santa Marta to the west.

He had to get to the plane faster than the winch could pull him. Rod reached down and unfastened the snap that held the line to his harness. Then, with hundreds of pounds of pressure behind each clenched fist as it closed, he began to make his way, hand over hand, toward the Hercules transport.

There was only one problem. The readout for power consumption in his visual display now read fourteen percent, and hand-walking up the line this way would use power at a terrific rate. As he watched, the four changed to a three.

But there ought to be enough to make the trip, with a small bit of reserve.

He kept moving, battling the wind and the drag of his own body.

"We're over the water," Smolleck yelled.

"Give it a moment," Gallagher replied. "I don't want any bodies washing ashore." He walked aft a few paces, peering back at the robot. His eyes widened. The damn thing was hauling itself toward the plane, coming hand over hand! "I'll be fucked," he muttered. "Hey, Smolleck! Give me your knife!" He handed the pistol to Smolleck. "Watch him."

Knife in hand, he started forward. The nylon line ran through the slot in the deck forward to where it engaged the slow-turning drum of the winch. If he cut the line, the robot would fall.

And there'd be no danger of that thing washing

ashore. It would sink like a stone, miles off the Colombian coast.

Rod saw Smolleck hand Gallagher a combat knife, saw the CIA EXDIR walking toward the winch. There was nothing he could do about it, however, except pull himself along more quickly.

Thirty more yards to go.

Power reading eight percent.

Drake was handcuffed, but his feet weren't tied. He knew he couldn't take the time to get his hands in front of him, as he had the last time he'd found himself in this position, but he might not need them. Navy SEALs train extensively in the martial arts form called hwrang-do.

His immediate problem was Smolleck, who was standing close by, a silenced Smith & Wesson automatic in his hand. He would have to take the gunman down before he could deal with Gallagher, and he had to do it *now*.

He gauged the distance between himself and Smolleck's feet. The logistics man had misjudged and stepped just a bit too close.

Timing his move with the motion of the aircraft, Drake rolled suddenly toward Smolleck, lashing his feet out in a hard double scissors, locking his ankles around Smolleck's calves and continuing the roll, knocking the CIA man off balance.

"Watch out!" the man screamed, and then the gun went off as he fell, the noise sharp and loud despite the sound suppressor, punching a neat round hole in a first-aid locker on the bulkhead. The gun clattered across the deck.

Drake lurched to his feet, drew back, then snapped his right foot hard into the side of Smolleck's skull.

Gallagher spun, knife up. "You're more trouble than you're worth, Navy," he said. He turned slightly and clicked the switch that controlled the winch to off. "Why don't you step outside with your friend?"

He advanced with the knife.

Drake stepped aside as Gallagher lunged at him. He knew better than to try kicking the knife; he could tell by the way the CIA man moved that he'd been trained in close combat, and lashing out with his foot would only get him stabbed . . . and probably incapacitated. Instead Drake lunged feetfirst at Gallagher's feet, imitating the move of a baseball player sliding into home plate. His feet locked around Gallagher's ankles. A hard snap-twist and roll sent EXDIR crashing against the aircraft's bulkhead. Quickly, he jerked his feet clear and scrambled upright, looking for a chance to end the fight.

He was too slow . . . or simply unlucky. Gallagher had dropped the knife when he hit but was already clawing across the deck toward the pistol, now lying only a few feet away. Drake took a step forward, then stopped. Gallagher stood five feet away, crouched over, the Smith & Wesson aimed at Drake's chest.

"Good-bye, SEAL . . ."

Rod had kept climbing the rope even after the winch was shut down and had almost reached the end of the aircraft's open tail ramp. In the lee of the Hercules, the air was calmer. Clinging with one hand to the line, he reached out with the other, clamping down on the end of the ramp.

His power reserves were down to five percent.

He would never make it back aboard now. He knew that. Perhaps, though, he could still save Chris Drake. All he needed was a projectile of some sort. . . .

Closing his left elbow over the line, he locked it tight with five hundred pounds' pressure. Swinging wildly, buffeted by the wind, a yard from the cargo ramp, he reached with his right hand to his left, peeling back an armored access, releasing a clamp, severing electrical connections. The fingers of his left hand closed into a fist, then froze as he lost all sensory input from it. He severed another connection, then quickly unscrewed his left hand from his arm. The thing came away in his right hand, still tight-closed, a lump of steel literally the size of his fist.

Still locked to the line by the pressure exerted by his left arm, he drew back with his right, targeting the back of Gallagher's head. He had to wait for a fraction of a second, calculating his body's uncertain motions on the end of the line, the wind pressure, the range. . . .

He would have only the one shot.

Rod's right arm snapped out and forward. The steel fist struck Gallagher at the base of his neck with the crunching sound of splintering bone. EXDIR's arms and legs splayed out as though he'd been jolted by an electric shock, then he crumpled forward, the Smith & Wesson dropping from nerveless fingers.

The robot's right hand scrabbled at the end of the ramp. His power level read one percent.

It wasn't enough. . . .

Drake was past Gallagher before the former EXDIR's body hit the deck, dropping onto his belly as he tried to reach Rod across the slanting surface of the ramp. He caught his breath as he looked down into blue water far, far below. The wind tore at his clothing, his hair. His hands closed on Rod's hand, where it clung to the metal grating of the ramp.

He tried to pull and nearly pulled himself out of the aircraft. He would never be able to haul Rod's three-hundred-pound-plus body onto the plane.

The line.

"Hold on with your right hand!" he yelled at the robot. "Let go of the line!"

"Power . . . going . . ." Rod replied. The two words seemed to exhaust him. His left arm unfolded, and the line fluttered free in the breeze.

Drake pulled in two forearm-lengths of nylon, looping it around Rod's right wrist and snugging it into a fisherman's bend.

Then he was scrambling back up the ramp, knees shaking with exertion. He reached the winch and switched it on.

Slowly, metal grating on metal, Rod was drawn into the aircraft. Drake hit the "cargo door close" lever, then ran back to where Rod lay legless, helpless, face up on the deck.

"Thank . . . you . . . Chris . . ."

Drake collapsed beside the machine, the strength

gone from his legs now that the crisis was past. "Rod! Rod! Can you hear me?" There was no response, and Drake realized he was conserving power. "Listen to me! Thanks for taking down Gallagher. He would have had me if you hadn't jumped in."

The robot's eyes tracked, focusing on Drake's face. A strange sound came from Rod's throat, then words. Drake had to lean closer to make them out.

"It looked like . . . you needed . . . a . . . hand. . . ."

Epilogue

ROD WAS DEAD by the time the C-130 touched down at Homestead Air Force Base in Florida. Fortunately for the RAMROD prototype, death was a correctable malfunction. A trickle charge from on-board emergency power packs kept his memory intact when all other systems shut down. At Camp Peary, the RAMROD team was ready to transplant his core units into Civilian Mod.

Function nominal.

It wasn't until he joined Drake and Weston in a subterranean conference room at RAMROD headquarters days later that he learned what had happened after his return.

The Salazars had, indeed, escaped the bloodbath at the hacienda. Colombian government troops, alerted by Group Seven, had descended on the compound within hours of the battle, discovering forty-two bodies, nearly three tons of cocaine stored in a warehouse near the airfield, and enough arms and munitions to fight a small war. The soldiers were tracking the survivors through the jungle.

But the Salazars were gone. A small aircraft had

been tracked leaving the airfield shortly after the battle, heading toward the interior.

AMBER HARVEST, however, was an unqualified success. The rogue faction within the CIA had been broken, and Diamond himself was dead. Delgado was a prisoner, as was Smolleck—assuming the former CIA logistics man recovered from his fractured skull. Background checks on those two suggested that Gallagher had begun dealing in drugs ten years earlier, back when he was still the head of CIA logistics. The man who arranged flights in and out of countries all over the world, who dealt with criminal elements, who had to strike deals with everyone from corrupt local officials to the Mafia, had found himself in a position of supreme temptation.

And the maze of security and need-to-know restrictions had made it easy to use the system to create his own inner circle of corruption and greed. Delgado and Smolleck were expected to lead Group Seven to quite a few others like themselves, government officials ensnared by billions in narcodollars, by the power those billions could purchase.

"We're never going to get them all," Drake said, shaking his head. "The whole thing seems pretty hopeless, you know? I mean, three *tons* of coke captured in that warehouse . . . and it's just a drop in the bucket. In the *ocean* . . ."

"Annual consumption of cocaine in the United States alone is estimated at five hundred tons," Rod said. "The drugs seized at the Salazar estate represents six-tenths of one percent of that amount."

"So we didn't even make a dent in it."

"You did better than *dent* it," Weston said. "You destroyed the Salazar operation, put them out of business."

"They got away."

"You wrecked their pipeline into Washington. You know, your friend Delgado is telling us an interesting story. About how the Salazars were planning on using their CIA connections to ship the stuff on U.S. military transports into military bases."

"Oh, God, no . . ."

"They'd already sent one ton through. Thanks to Delgado's information, the DEA went into a warehouse outside of Andrews and grabbed most of it . . . along with twelve members of the *Salvajes* motorcycle gang who were dealing the stuff in the D.C. area."

"That's something, anyway."

"Something? One metric ton. That's a lot of doses. A hell of a lot of kids getting hooked on the stuff their first or second time they play with it, babies addicted inside the womb, first-time users looking for a high and ending up dead. Yeah, that's something.

"And I'll tell you another thing. Our nation is in serious trouble, and it's not just the cokeheads and crack houses and rising crime and gun battles in the street that's doing it. It's the corruption. Drugs and drug money foul everything they touch . . . and they've touched plenty in this country already. Including some highly placed people inside the Washington Beltway. Delgado has told us a lot about *them*, too."

"Who?"

"The DEA is working on them. It'll take time, like a surgeon working on a very persistent, very deep-seated tumor. It has to come out, but the cancer has infected so much of the rest of the body . . ."

"The patient could die," Drake said softly.

"Yes, it could," Weston said. "The surgeon is going to have to be ruthless."

"Is there any chance at all?"

"We think so. Group Seven . . . and the President. You see, we can only do so much trying to close our borders. People like the Salazars and the Ochoas and the Sicilian Mafia and God knows who else are going to keep shipping the stuff in, so long as there's a market for it here. And humans being what they are, there will *always* be a market. . . ."

"So what's the alternative?"

"We can strike back. Like that surgeon's scalpel . . . cut out the tumor before it destroys the patient. Before it destroys us." Weston's eyes moved from Drake to the robot, and back. "And you two—you and Rod—can help."

"That sounds suspiciously like a proposition."

"If you like. Group Seven was impressed by the way Rod handled himself in Colombia. He could play a part in hitting the drug lords where they live."

"Why me?"

"Because you know Rod. You work well with him." Weston grinned. "Because, so help me, the two of you *think* alike."

Drake looked at Rod and grinned. "You want me to be his keeper?"

"Well, like Dr. McDaniels says, he still has some trouble getting along in a human world. In acting human, *being* human . . . though from what I've seen, he's well on his way. What do you say? Want the job?"

No one asked Rod what he thought, but that didn't matter. He already knew what Chris Drake's answer was going to be, knew the part they would have to play. . . .

Drake thought about it. Nothing could bring back Meagan or Stacy. The pain was still there, part of him, like a robot's programming, a nightmare that went on and on.

But the nightmare was not his alone. Drug lords, monsters in human form, were growing rich by selling wholesale misery and slavery and death to men, women, and children by the thousands, by the *millions*.

They had to be stopped.

He looked at the robot, knowing he'd found a partner there, someone he could trust.

Someone who, machine or not, *felt* as he did.

He extended his hand toward Weston. "Count me in," he said.

He could help . . . with the help of a robot called Cybernarc.

Robert Cain is the pseudonym of an author who lives in Pennsylvania.

HarperPaperbacks *By Mail*

NIGHT STALKERS by *Duncan Long*. TF160, an elite helicopter corps, is sent into the Caribbean to settle a sizzling private war.

NIGHT STALKERS— SHINING PATH by *Duncan Long*. The Night Stalkers help the struggling Peruvian government protect itself from terrorist attacks until America's Vice President is captured by the guerillas and all diplomatic tables are turned.

NIGHT STALKERS— GRIM REAPER by *Duncan Long*. This time TF160 must search the dead-cold Antarctic for a renegade nuclear submarine.

NIGHT STALKERS— DESERT WIND by *Duncan Long*. The hot sands of the Sahara blow red with centuries of blood. Night Stalkers are assigned to transport a prince safely across the terrorist-teeming hell.

TROPHY by *Julian Jay Savarin*. Hand-picked pilots. A futuristic fighter plane. A searing thriller about the ultimate airborne confrontation.

STRIKE FIGHTERS— SUDDEN FURY by *Tom Willard* The Strike Fighters fly on the cutting edge of a desperate global mission—a searing military race to stop a fireball of terror.

STRIKE FIGHTERS—BOLD FORAGER by *Tom Willard*. Sacrette and his Strike Fighters battle for freedom in this heart-pounding, modern-day adventure.

STRIKE FIGHTERS: WAR CHARIOT by *Tom Willard*. Commander Sacrette finds himself deep in a bottomless pit of international death and destruction. Players in the world-wide game of terrorism emerge, using fear, shock and sex as weapons.